About the Author

John Thompson was born in Lancashire in 1942. He served in 16 Parachute Brigade and 22 SAS Regiment. Since his retirement he has walked up to Everest Base Camp, ran several marathons and ultra marathons, has become a Black Belt martial arts exponent and now lives with his wife in Anglesey, North Wales.

And the Regiment Blind with Dust and Smoke
(And other non-PC Military tales from the last 50 years)

Compiled and written by John Thompson
Ex-Special Forces
(With a little help from his friends)

Profit received from sales of this book will go to military charity No. 1121647: The Afghanistan Trust

John Thompson

And the Regiment Blind with Dust and Smoke

Olympia Publishers
London

www.olympiapublishers.com
OLYMPIA PAPERBACK EDITION

Copyright © John Thompson 2014

The right of John Thompson to be identified as author of
this work has been asserted in accordance with sections 77 and 78 of the
Copyright, Designs and Patents Act 1988.

All Rights Reserved

No reproduction, copy or transmission of this publication
may be made without written permission.
No paragraph of this publication may be reproduced,
copied or transmitted save with the written permission of the publisher, or in
accordance with the provisions
of the Copyright Act 1956 (as amended).

Any person who commits any unauthorised act in relation to
this publication may be liable to criminal
prosecution and civil claims for damage.

A CIP catalogue record for this title is
available from the British Library.

ISBN: 978-1-84897-435-7

(Olympia Publishers is part of Ashwell Publishing Ltd)

First Published in 2014

Olympia Publishers
60 Cannon Street
London
EC4N 6NP

Printed in Great Britain

**IN MEMORY
OF ALL THE SERVICEMEN I KNEW
WHO HAVE DIED SERVING GREAT BRITAIN**

*The sand of the desert is sodden red
Red with the blood of a square that broke
The Gatling's jammed and the Colonel's dead
And the Regiment blind with dust and smoke*

*The river of death has brimmed his banks
And England's far, and Honour a name
But the voice of a school boy rallies the ranks:
"Play up! Play up! And play the game!"*

Vitai Lampada (They Pass On The Torch of Life), Sir Henry Newbolt (1862-1938)

Acknowledgements

With thanks and acknowledgement to all the contributors who have given me permission to put their stories in the book and who have helped make my Military years the best of my life. Their initials are shown after their story/anecdote.

I would like to give particular acknowledgement for his help and contribution to Jim Davidson OBE, comedian and a good friend of the Military. I would also like to add special thanks to Chip Wood, the Soldier Magazine cartoonist, whose cartoons brighten up the book. The PRA (West Berkshire Branch) for their kind donation, and finally to Nick T for his extremely generous donation towards the publication costs.

CONTENTS

IN THE 1960S   17
1   19
    JOHNNY KID AND THE PIRATES
2   21
    PARACHUTING – 1960S STYLE
3   23
    THE BUDGIE
4   25
    WEAPON TRAINING – HOW NOT TO DO IT
5   27
    WHO SAID BALLOON JUMPS WERE BORING?
6   30
    SET A THIEF TO CATCH A THEIF
7   32
    THE GRAND NATIONAL (MY ONE AND ONLY WINNER)
8   34
    SERGEANT MAJORS – TENDER WORDS AND ACTIONS
9   37
    ALCOHOL AND ME! – LIBYA 1968
10   39
    SCRAP METAL – 9 PARA SQN RE
11   41
    AIRBOURNE TRAINING – MEMORIES OF ENLISTMENT AND TRAINING
12   47
    CYPRUS – NEW YEARS DAY 1964
13   49
    THE DAY CHARLIE WATTS THREW A WOBBLER
14   56
    WHEN "HAPPY HOUR" CAME EARLY
15   58
    A "FIREY" DAY IN JUNE
16   70
    PULLING THE FLAG DOWN

17	72
DOBBIE'S BUCKSHEE STEAK AND KIDNEY PIE	
18	75
THE HANDOVER PARADE	
19	77
16 PARA HY DROP COMPANY RAOC WATCHFIELD	
20	78
TRUE LOVE (WITH AN EXPLOSIVE ENDING)	
21	83
A VERY LUCKY PARACHUTIST	

IN THE 1970s — 87

22	89
SOUTH KOREA	
23	94
FORGIVE BUT DO NOT FORGET	
24	95
PARACHUTING – THE MAYOR OF GRAYS, ESSEX	
25	97
PARACHUTING – BSM YORKIE CHALLINOR 7 PARA REGT RHA	
26	98
SURVEILLANCE – THE GOLDEN RULES	
27	100
PARACHUTING – OPERATION DROP OUT	
28	101
LET ME ENTERTAIN YOU	
29	103
TO CRACK A NUT	
30	104
RHEINDAHLEN HOLIDAY CAMP – DRINKING AND NOT DRIVING	
31	105
SOLDIERS AND CREDIT	
32	107
THE MINEFIELD GAP BAOR	
33	109
THE GUARDSMAN'S BURDEN	

34	110
WEETABIX	
35	111
A CRY IN THE DARK	
36	113
A FALLEN HERO	
37	116
THE LEGACY OF THE BRITISH RAJ	
IN THE 1980s	119
38	121
MY FIRST ENCOUNTER WITH SPECIAL FORCES JIM DAVIDSON OBE	
39	126
MEMORIES FROM THE IRANIAN EMBASSY SIEGE, LONDON 1980	
40	130
SURVEILLANCE	
41	132
A COMEDIAN WHO WASN'T IN THE ARMY JIM DAVIDSON OBE, BELIZE	
42	135
MARRIED MEN – AND THEIR WIVES	
43	136
SOLDIERS – MISBEHAVING	
44	138
HEADQUARTERS BRITISH FORCES HONG KONG	
45	139
BEING A PARATROOPER	
46	140
THE OMAN IN THE 1980s (A SOLDIER IN THE POLICE)	
47	144
THE FALKLANDS – PASS ROYAL!	
48	145
PHYSICAL TRAINING ON RFA SIR BEDIVERE – STAR JUMPS	

IN THE 1990s — 147
49 — 149
   WHEN ONE'S HEAD IS ON THE BLOCK
50 — 151
   DIVING WITH GADGET MAN
51 — 153
   DIVING GALLIPOLI

IN THE NEW MILLENIUM — 155
52 — 157
   FALKLANDS RETURN 2008 – MISTAKEN IDENTITY
53 — 160
   I SOLD MY MEDALS YESTERDAY
54 — 162
   SOLD AND GONE!
55 — 168
   FALKLANDS RETURN 2008 – WITH THE GUARDS
56 — 170
   THE NOBEL PEACE PRIZE 1991 (AND WHERE'S OUR MONEY?)
57 — 172
   ALWAYS A LITTLE FURTHER BUT NOT TOO FAR – EVEREST 2010
58 — 174
   I WANT MY COLD WAR BACK
59 — 177
   GETTING THERE IN THE END!
60 — 181
   P A R A v M A R I N E

IN THE 1960s

1
JOHNNY KIDD AND THE PIRATES

In May 1962, Aldershot was the home of the British Army and also 16 Parachute Brigade. We were young then and enjoyed life to the full, which meant the public houses in the town were always crowded. We trained hard and drank hard! I remember one Friday when my mate Mick Marshall a Para cook, later a Colonel in the Army Catering Corps and I went out to celebrate his 21st birthday. We began the inevitable pub crawl and after about five different pubs we landed in "The Rat Pit" which was normally our local. After a drink there Mick, although slightly under the weather, remembered that the Army Catering Corps Depot had a Grand Dance on that night and that a decent group were playing there. We decided to go and we drove there, "drinking and driving" never seemed wrong in those days.

We went in to the dance hall and the place was really rocking with hundreds on the dance floor and the group playing at 1,000 decibels, as normal! Johnny Kidd and the Pirates were quite well known and all wore complete pirate dress with Johnny wearing an eye patch over his right eye. They had recently had a hit called *Shakin' All Over* and were now belting out their latest and as it later turned out, very appropriate song, *Please Don't Touch*. We had another drink and Mick, who had drank a lot more than me, decided out of the blue to go on stage and tell everyone it was his 21st birthday.

Mick staggered onto the stage and attempted to wrestle the mike from Johnny Kidd and announce his birthday but Mr

Kidd had different ideas. He was obviously taking the *Please Don't Touch* bit to heart. He hit Mick who promptly fell off the stage and collapsed on the floor. I, having had a few drinks, was incensed by this treatment of my best friend, jumped onto the stage and with a lucky punch knocked Johnny Kidd into his drummer's drums. All hell broke out then as I think most who were there had gone with the "the next dance will be a fight" syndrome anyway. The ending to all this was I grabbed Mick, got him to my car and on driving away, looked back and saw the Orderly Officer and six of the Guard running into what was now a clear riot.

The funny part is that Johnny Kidd spent at least the next two weeks with the patch over his other eye!

—JT

2
PARACHUTING – 1960s STYLE

Father Hughie Beattie was 16 Parachute Brigade's RC priest in the 1960s. He was full of fun and greeted everyone with a big smile and was never too busy to stop and chat with anyone, irrespective of rank or status.

I recall an amusing incident at RAF Odiham in Hampshire. Odiham was often used as the mounting airfield for parachute exercises and I remember one summer's evening, hundreds of paratroopers in orderly lines fitting parachutes before emplaning for a night drop onto Salisbury Plain.

A 'stick' of soldiers, including Hughie Beattie, trundled past wearing parachutes and carrying their weapons containers on their shoulders. These containers would typically carry a soldier's personal and fighting equipment including his rifle. For non-operational (i.e. continuation) training, it was not uncommon for men to pack a jerrican full of water in the container. This had the dual advantage of meeting the weight criterion of 45lbs and could be emptied immediately after landing thereby avoiding the hassle of carrying a heavy container a mile or two. However, following a near-fatality involving a jettisoned jerrican, the practice of using this form of ballast was banned by our dear friends, the RAF.

It was clear from the look of Hughie's container, that he either had not read the instruction banning jerricans or he had chosen to ignore it. When one of my stick spotted Hughie's container, he shouted "Hey Father don't you know the Crabs[1] have banned jerricans?" to which Hughie promptly replied, "Holy water my son. God bless you."

—PO'C

---

[1] Crab was the Navy and Army slang for the RAF first coined by the RN as the colour of RAF uniforms was reminiscent of "crab oil" the nickname of the paint used on warships. It has nothing to do with the allegation, rife in the Army, that the RAF walk sidewards!

3
THE BUDGIE

Way back in the late 1960s, two enterprising soldiers from nine Parachute Squadron Royal Engineers found themselves short of money during a long hot summer leave from their unit based in Aldershot.

At that time, Southern Gas was deep into a programme to convert domestic users' homes from traditional coal gas to natural gas and there was therefore a continual demand for engineers. The urgency to complete the programme meant that anyone with any basic engineering nous could blag a job. With this in mind, our boys pitched up at the local Gas Depot and within the hour found themselves each with a gas fitter's toolkit and a list of properties to convert.

In fairness, the boys did have a degree of skill and were very soon in the swing and by lunchtime, had completed almost a day's worth of conversions. They felt that they had earned a break and eased their way to the "Ratpit" (at the time a favourite Para pub in Aldershot) for a pork pie and a few pints.

After lunch, they tackled the last house of the day that was owned by an old widow who welcomed them with a brew. Having set the boys up with a nice cup of tea, the widow announced that she had some shopping to do and would be out for an hour.

The lads got stuck in to the job and in no time had finished and having packed away their tools were about to knock off for the day when they noticed in the birdcage in the corner a small yellow budgerigar lying flat on its back, stone dead.

Now because natural gas is odourless, the boys figured that the poor budgie had succumbed through gas poisoning. Shit, they thought. How were they to break news to the old dear? After a quick brainstorming it was decided, using thick soldering wire, to secure the budgie to its perch in a lifelike pose. This was a delicate procedure that involved inserting two inches of the wire up the bird's bum and with the rest of the wire, carefully wrapped around its feet to secure it to the perch. Job done, the lads headed for the door hoping to escape before the widow returned.

On opening the door to make their exit, they were greeted by the widow who bustled them back into room. Just as the boys were about to confess the widow blurted out "Bloody hell, what's happened to the budgie, he's been dead for two weeks!" Phew!

—PO'C

4
WEAPON TRAINING – HOW NOT TO DO IT

In mid 1967 as a young, airborne, private soldier I attended a military training course at a certain RAOC depot. This involved the usual military skills of drill, weapon training, fitness, map reading, etc.

Coming from an airborne unit I did this training every week, unlike some of my new course colleagues from non airborne units.

The course consisted of 15 junior NCOs and Ptes from various units. I was the only airborne soldier. One glorious summer's day we all sat outside, in a semi-circle, in front of the instructor for a weapon training lesson. I was sat on the extreme left of this semi-circle.

The Sgt instructor had forgotten, or never had, a rifle cleaning kit. However, he proceeded with the lesson, disassembling, cleaning and reassembling the SLR. When he reached the cleaning part he began by saying, "In my hand you will have to imagine I am holding a rifle cleaning kit". He then proceeded to "clean" the weapon with his imaginary kit!

When it was the students turn to teach the lesson, the instructor fortunately started at the opposite end to where I was sitting. Each student stood up in front of the class and stated, quite happily, "For this part of the lesson you will have to imagine I am holding a rifle cleaning kit".

I couldn't wait! One by one all 14 of them did the same drill. When my turn came, I stood in front of the class, put right hand in right hand pouch, pulled out a little metal box and proudly stated, "In my unit everyone is issued with one of these"!

The airborne soldier left the course as top student!

—DG

5
WHO SAID BALLOON JUMPS WERE BORING?

Though most paratroopers preferred the hustle and bustle of leaping from a noisy and smelly Hercules aircraft to the rather cold-blooded stepping into fresh air from a captive balloon cage, balloon jumping open days were a staple recruiting tool for the units of HQ 16 Para Bde.

Standard format was that the visiting party, typically of schoolboys or young soldiers, would be bussed down to Hankley Common to be met by an RAF Safety Team, a tethered balloon, a pile of parachutes and a few doughty volunteers winkled out of their offices into the bright sunshine to perform for the visitors. Each cage would be filled with three of the visiting party, kitted out with parachute and reserve in case the balloon broke free, one RAF dispatcher and one jumper. Up would go the balloon; out would jump our brave airborne warrior basking in the adulation of the visitors; and the cage would then be winched in to disembark the visitors and take on the next group.

This would generally continue uneventfully until the pile of parachutes had been used up or the visitors became visibly bored after several trips up in the balloon.

Not all such days, however, were completely uneventful. On one particular occasion, an open day had been arranged by the Royal Army Pay Corps and, because they were short of para trained personnel, G C and I were "volunteered" from the Bde HQ to make up the jumping numbers.

Everything was set fair on the day with Hankley Common resplendent in early summer sunshine. The first few trips went strictly to plan until all the visitors had done at least one trip up in the balloon cage. Then because there was still a fairly large pile of parachutes to get through, we started to change the format for some lifts with two jumpers going up at a time and leaping out.

Alas, as those familiar with Murphy's Law are aware "Anything that can go wrong, will go wrong", it does not do to tinker with routine. Suddenly, the peace and tranquillity of Hankley Common was pierced by a high pitched scream and we looked up to see two parachutes in the sky, the lower one was properly dressed in boots and Dennison smock and getting into position for the standard heels, arse, head landing while the other was clearly in school uniform with arms and legs flailing like some demented octopus.

At this point, the young RAF DZ Safety Officer, seeing his career pass in front of his eyes, leapt into action and rushed about the DZ with his megaphone screaming, "Get your feet and knees together" and "Tuck your elbows in" while other members of the RAF ground crew ran towards the expected landing point adding their encouragement. Other military personnel on the ground in true professional fashion fell about laughing.

As with all good stories, it ended well. Our young hero bounced in the heather with no real damage done and after getting disentangled from the harness strutted his stuff, revelling in the hero worship of his peers and no doubt still dining out on it today.

Who said balloon jumps were boring?

—DL

"Ponsonby Minor?... Get back in that balloon or it's detention for you my lad!"

6
SET A THIEF TO CATCH A THIEF

Until 1965, HQ 16 Parachute Brigade plus some minor Brigade units were located at Elles Barracks in Farnborough, Hampshire. As was the norm then, army camps would 'mount' a guard to provide low level security during 'silent' hours (i.e. evening and weekends). So it was that on one windy, wet, late autumn evening my mate, a full corporal, found himself in the role of Brigade HQ Guard Commander. This was one of the most boring duties on the planet with little or no sleep, crap food and rubbish TV. Rarely, very rarely, an interesting incident might occur to break the monotony. Just after midnight, my pal was having a nap when he was woken to take a phone call from the Hampshire Constabulary control room. The message was that one of their patrol cars had been passing the Brigade HQ ammunition store, known as the magazine, and spotted a couple of characters on the roof – obviously up to no good. As the civilian police had no responsibility for security of military property they swiftly handed the problem over to my mate who briefed two of the resting soldiers to arm themselves to the teeth and make haste to the magazine, investigate and report back. So, armed with that trusty weapon of choice (a pick handle!), the paratroopers made their way on tip toes to the scene of the crime. Upon arrival, they were surprised to see two of the guard, who were supposed to be on patrol, on the magazine roof quietly stripping off the best part of half a ton of lead. After a brief discussion and an agreement to split the proceeds four ways, the two intrepid investigators returned to the guard room. "Don't know what the Old Bill is on about Corp, we never saw nuffin goin' on at the magazine". Oh what a Band of Brothers.

—PO'C

7
THE GRAND NATIONAL (MY ONE AND ONLY WINNER)

As I had to leave the UK very quickly in the mid Sixties having smashed my Mini Cooper and owing a local garage the hire purchase cost of it, the 2IC of my unit sent me to the Trucial Oman Scouts based near Sharjah in the Trucial Oman States. The idea being that I could recover physically and financially serving there out-of-the-way! Sharjah was a very small town and Dubai was virtually a creek in the mid-Sixties. How times have changed: Sharjah and Dubai are large, rich towns, the Trucial Oman States is now the United Arab Emirates and the Trucial Oman Scouts no longer exist. I arrived at the Camp the day the Grand National was being run in the UK and on entering the Sgts mess to report to the RSM, I noticed a Sweepstake was being held for the race. The RSM after acknowledging me, requested I buy a ticket, which I willingly did! He being the RSM! I then had a couple of drinks and headed back to my new room as the alcohol and the journey I had undertaken were taking their toll. I lay on the bed and "crashed out!" I was woken, very rudely, by the RSM hammering on the door, entering the room and thrusting a huge wad of foreign notes in my hand. I gathered that the horse I had backed, Red Alligator, had won and the RSM stressed, as they do, that it was customary to buy a round of drinks in the bar when in this situation. I took the money, and the hint, and wandered back to the Mess still only half awake. Everyone seemed to be at the bar so I bought the drinks for all and after I had had a couple more drinks, thought it was a good idea to buy them all again! And a little later, again! I cannot remember anymore other than waking up 24 hrs later, flat out on my bed, with not a penny (or a Dirham as it was there) to my name!

To this day, I do not know how much I had won and spent but I do know that I had made a lot of "friends" very quickly!

—JT

8
SERGEANT MAJORS – TENDER WORDS AND ACTIONS

(ONE)
Scene, parade square Aldershot 1968. Whole unit on parade practising drill for forthcoming annual fitness for role inspection. Soldiers in single file, about to form three ranks. CSM, standing thirty yards away across the square; "From the left, "NUMBER!" Number thirteen happened to be one LCpl G. As he called his number, the CSM screamed "HALT! Back to 13." LCpl G, why were you absent from the ranges last night?" LCpl G. "My wife is in hospital, Sir, expecting a baby, and I was excused". Remember the CSM is thirty yards away whilst we have this "private" conversation in front of the whole unit. CSM "When is the baby due?" LCpl G "Last Sunday, Sir!" CSM "Have you reported her for being late!"

End of private conversation.

—DG

(TWO)
To a soldier who complained about being cold and wet on exercise "Smiff, yer skin's waterproof and if you keep yer bleeding mouth shut all yer bodily orifices are one-way valves!"

To an officer cadet standing on parade "Am I hurting you, Sir?" "No, Sir" "Well, I should be cos I'm standing on yer 'air!"

To a rather lacklustre soldier "Being a soldier, Smiff, is a case of mind over matter. I don't mind and you don't matter!"

—JM

(THREE)
An Intelligence Corps soldier serving with 16 Para Bde Int Platoon, when on a parade for best kit inspection was asked by the Sergeant Major if he had his BEST boots on. The soldier answered that they were NOT his best boots and when asked "why not", answered the Sergeant Major "because I do not believe in favouritism!" Unsurprisingly, the soldier was last seen being marched up the road at a vast rate of knots in the direction of the Guardroom!

—CB

(FOUR)
A Sergeant Major, (who shall remain nameless but this is nevertheless a true story), when on training parachute sorties took great delight in winding up young Sandhurst Officer Cadets who often came on the flights purely for air experience. On one particular flight, which I was on, the Sergeant Major took one look at a couple of baby faced cadets sitting directly opposite and observing that they were looking decidedly green around the gills, took a paper sick bag out of his pocket, put it up to his face and pretended to vomit into it! (The cadets, unsurprisingly, started to lose the colour in their faces). He then passed the bag to the chap sitting next to him who was obviously in on the scam. The cadets looked on in amazement and still looking confused, wondered if they should make their sick bags ready. Just then the chap in possession of the sick bag took a spoon out of his pocket, placed it inside the bag, spooned out the contents and

proceeded to eat them. Immediately two of the cadets were violently sick and continued to be so for the remainder of the flight! The Sergeant Major and his accomplice had succeeded in their mission. The cadets were, of course, unaware that his sick bag contained a small quantity of Compo (Airborne) Stew which was more than could be said about theirs!

—CB

9
ALCOHOL AND ME! – LIBYA 1968

Alcohol figured in many of my downfalls. In 1968 in Libya in a tented camp which 16 Para Bde ran as the Admin Base Unit, the ABU, for major exercises, I was a rather shiny new Lance Corporal. During an evening drinking session in our luxury beer tent, I for some unfathomable reason got into a heated discussion with Ossie, one of our chums who was possibly the biggest prop at that time in Corps rugby. A generally placid lad, he weighed in at around 16 stone and had unusually large hands. He was huge and we had set up a localised team that had another giant propping, one Dennis Priestley RMP, with me at Hooker. I couldn't hook for toffee but we were relying on crushing the opposition with our combined weights. I was a sylph-like 13 stone then. Ossie invited me outside the beer tent and I naively followed him out. One of his huge hams, termed 'fist', laid me out neatly on the deck. I woke up some eight hours later on my camp bed nursing a hangover, a split lip and seven stitches in the back of my head from where I had landed on a metal tent peg. I had no memory of any of it which made me a particularly unsuitable witness at his arraignment on the Monday morning. Major Weighill, Royal Horse Artillery presided and Sar'nt Major Danny Hadden PARA did the marching in and out. As Ossie could not clearly remember what happened either and as all the potential witnesses claimed to be inside the tent at the time, the 'trial' was a bit of a farce. The OC acknowledged that we were friends but the dignity of the rank of Lance Corporal had been challenged and this must be visibly punished. Ossie got seven days jankers. I got a lengthy and humbling ear bending from Danny Hadden. We were 20 miles from the coast and 100 miles from Tobruk. The resident Battalion there, The Royal Ulster Rifles, couldn't offer a place in their nick – (knowing the time and the place and the lads, it was probably full!). The RAF at El Adem wouldn't consider having anything as vulgar as a soldier in their pristine guardroom. Ossie, therefore, served his time in the ABU Guard Tent doing General Duty (GD) tasks. A length of mine tape "do not pass" line delineating his "cell". I think we sneaked him the odd beer of an evening! I shall remain anonymous save to those who were in the ABU!

—GC

10
SCRAP METAL – 9 PARA SQN RE

On occasion our Plant Troop got what they would say were nice little jobs, jobs that had more than one outcome. This was one of them. The Squadron was out of the country and I was left behind on rear party in order that I could assist with a move from QE Barracks in Crookham to the Barracks at Crookham Crossroads. During the march out I was showing a Captain from the incoming Ghurkha Rifles through the supposedly empty MT compound when we came across two badly shelled tank targets and some broken tank tracks. The Captain was not amused and gave me a right earful, ending by telling me that he would be back the next morning and that it had better not be there. (Fortunately, he was so angry he missed the rowing boat in the static water tank!) At that time we had a plant operator working out at the Training Regiment in Cove so I phoned and asked him if he knew about the old targets. The reply was they had been purloined from the tank ranges at Bovington with the intent that when flogged as scrap, they would provide a good "piss-up" for the lads. When I told him what had happened he agreed that it would be a good idea to get rid of them and offered to come across with a machine to load it into a three tonner and a low loader. He turned up, true to his word, and we loaded the metal onto the vehicles, The first target ripped up the floor of the lorry but luckily it belonged to the Training Regiment, not us, and when the other target was laid on the low loader, the wheels were almost on their rims. We headed for a scrap yard at North Camp (I believe it was known to our Plant Troop). It was an extremely slow journey and of course we had no Route Order. Anyway as we headed up Queens Avenue and opposite the Stadium, two Redcaps on horseback appeared on the other side of the road. They headed across towards us. We were petrified! They rode alongside us and got us to pull up and the nice Corporal said "where are you lads off to without an escort," I looked him in the eye as if we were all legit and said "to the Scrap Yard at North Camp", His reply was "you are moving very slow, we had better escort you there" and that they did without any further questions. So our convoy of two Military Police, two Horses, two weighed down vehicles and two young sappers (who wanted to be anywhere else but there), painfully made their way to North Camp! We got £90 for the scrap and on his return; a right bollocking from the Plant Sergeant – life in the Squadron was always interesting.

—BS

11
AIRBORNE TRAINING – MEMORIES OF ENLISTMENT AND TRAINING

"Why did you join the Paras?" I have often asked myself, but am not too clear on the answer. The Welsh tend to take education very seriously and I left school in 1959 with six "O" levels, including good old Mathematics and English. No great shakes nowadays, when so many have a university degree. But it was a reasonably significant achievement then and my father, a quarry labourer, was immensely proud that all his four children went to Grammar School. Others may have been more fortunate, but at no stage of my life can I claim to have had a clear vision of what I wanted to do. And this most certainly applied when I was a teenager. So the idea was to buy a bit of time by joining the Army. After a few years, I thought, I might be visited by an inspiration of what career path would suit me longer term. My father was aghast at this intention, and we did not speak for years.

Having decided to join, it rather came as news to me, on attending the recruiting office at Wrexham, that the Army was divided up into Regiments and Corps. I have only a vague recollection of why I chose the Paras. I seem to remember a rather fetching poster on the wall, portraying some very dashing characters in red berets. And the recruiting sergeant muttered something about extra pay, and a much better chance of serving abroad, which I found vaguely appealing. So joining the Paras was not a profoundly thought-out decision: I just drifted into it.

I distinctly remember the trauma of the journey, by rail, from Llanfairfechan to Aldershot. On arrival at Euston some spiv on the station concourse with a camera took my photo and told me that I owed him ten shillings. He was bullying and harassing and said it was too late to say that I didn't want a photograph and had no money anyway. Who did I think I was to have wasted his film? I eventually got away, handing over no money, but felt shaken by the episode.

On eventually arriving at Aldershot I was comforted to see an army truck waiting outside the station. I politely knocked on the window. "My name is Malcolm Rowlands", I said "are you waiting to collect me?" The RASC driver looked at me with total disdain, took a long drag on his Woodbine, said "Fuck off squaddie" and returned to his comic. So I felt crushed for a second time within a couple of hours. So I tramped up Hospital Hill and presented myself at the training depot, but for the life of me cannot be sure of the name of the barracks. I think it may have been Maida. By this time it was quite late, and having been travelling all day, I was starving hungry. I was issued with bedding, a mug and eating irons and directed towards the cookhouse. "What do you want mate?" said the friendly cook at the hotplate "we've got fish or airborne chicken."

"Chicken, please" I replied with enthusiasm: and was then dismayed when he put corned beef on my plate. I did not know, of course, that airborne chicken was then the current cookhouse slang for corned beef. It is strange how things have rather reversed over the years. Chicken was expensive and a comparative delicacy then; corned beef was commonplace. It used to be said that army cooks had thirty-nine recipes for corned beef, and that to pass the Catering Corps trade test you had to demonstrate an ability to cock up forty of them. I cannot remember precisely how many there were in my intake platoon. But I believe it was around forty, and this figure was reduced to around a dozen over the ten weeks of initial training. Not too much about the toughness of the course should be read into these bare facts. I reckon that a good half of airborne recruits were no-hopers from the outset: city lads who could scarcely run a mile without difficulty. Those who really wanted to get through did get through – not necessarily at the first attempt, and maybe after back-squadding through injury. One thing I did note, however: the brash and loud John Wayne types were rarely among those who passed muster. The Paras have always seemed to favour quiet determination as a characteristic rather than lots of fuss, false bravado and noise. Nearly all in the intake platoon were teenagers, but there was one elderly recruit aged twenty-five. We used to talk about him in the evenings, musing over how the hell anyone that old could expect to get through. But pass with us he did. A very early feature of recruit training, probably the first day, was a platoon haircut. On being told that this would take place during the hour or so between NAAFI break and lunch, I thought there must be several barbers to cater for around forty recruits. But Paddy-the-Chop, as he was affectionately known, worked entirely alone. Paddy would have won no prizes for artistic merit; but you certainly could not fault him for speed. As a teenager I was blessed with natural fitness and I honestly do not recall being fazed or troubled with many of the physical pursuits. In my native Wales I had roamed freely over the mountains from the age of about ten, and I represented the school at cross-country both as a junior and a senior. It was also an advantage to weigh about half what I am now. The hardest physical test for recruits was, to my mind at least, the dreaded log race. The logs were full-length telegraph poles, kept in water to give them extra weight. Teams of six or eight recruits would then be attached to the pole with their toggle ropes and race with the logs in knee-deep mud over the tank tracks or, worse, up to the trig point. The exercise was soon completely exhausting, and to some degree I think it was as much a psychological test as physical one. As it became more tiring it was very easy to convince yourself that someone in the team may not be pulling their weight. It would have been all too easy to take a breather and merely pretend to be pulling your hardest. One log-race was against outsiders: teams of officer cadets from Sandhurst. Our PTI – I cannot remember his name, but he was about five foot high and about the same distance across the shoulders, making him look like a muscular triangle that you would not want to tangle with. He growled in his barely understandable Glaswegian accent that we would be failed the course and sent home in disgrace if we allowed ourselves to be beaten by any "poofter Rupert crap-hats." This expression meant absolutely nothing to me at the time, but we thought it prudent to heed his advice and did not dare lose the race. In recent years there has been much in the media about the bullying of army recruits. I have searched my memory for any recollection of bullying during training. But there was absolutely none that I saw. It just was not the culture of the day. Our training NCOs were scarcely shrinking violets, but would have seen it as pathetic and unthinkable to abuse their considerable authority by any form of bullying. At the end of the ten weeks those of us who survived found ourselves at RAF Abingdon. We were there for a month, and billeted at Nearby Culham. The course was excellent and a real adventure, with one PJI (parachute jumping instructor) assigned to each section of eight. I have very fond memories of RAF Sergeant Charlie Dodds. At the age of 18 I looked about 15, and Charlie looked after me like a father. After the couple of weeks of ground training we were marched to the tethered balloon for our first jumps. Charlie's greeting on marshalling us into the balloon cage may be lost on anyone unfamiliar with crude airborne slang – or indeed anyone unfamiliar with pre-decimal currency.

But he beamed at us and said: "I bet I know what your ring-pieces are doing. Sixpence half-crown! Sixpence half-crown!" And he then cackled at his own joke. We did two balloon jumps: one via the door and the second through the aperture. Charlie had the same method with all first jumps. Up to when we were stood in the door, all instructions would be whispered gently and quietly very closely into our ears. But then he would suddenly bellow, "GO!" at the top of his voice, and we would shoot out of the balloon entirely automatically, the drill having been engrained during the repetitive ground training. Charlie was much amused by the way that first-jumpers would cling on to the balloon cage structure with white knuckles and like grim death when moving forward to the door. He saw this mortal fear of falling out as particularly pointless when you were about to jump out anyway. When back in the training hangar after our first jump, Charlie mimicked a demonstration of what we looked like. During his performance he fell about with helpless laughter at his own acting. Our amusement was rather more restrained, but we laughed along with him politely as a show of good manners. Six aircraft jumps followed: three from Hastings and three from Beverleys – one of which was from the upper deck aperture. Three were clean-fatigue, and three with containers. The last was a night drop. I remember distinctly the passing out parade at Abingdon, when we were presented with our wings by the Commanding Officer. I cannot remember his name, but I distinctly recall one sentence in his speech: "From this day forward, for the rest of your lives, every one of you will always be either a Para or an ex-Para". One vivid memory of the Abingdon course had nothing to do with parachuting. After a night out at Abingdon, and two or three pints of scrumpy (ie almost a fatal dose) it became our practice to swim naked in the Emergency Water Supply (EWS) tanks at Culham. The challenge was to dive in and swim under water to the other side, a distance of about fifteen yards. Bearing in mind that this was stagnant and weed-choked water, it is a miracle that none of us drowned or caught cholera. After Abingdon, we returned to Aldershot for a further six weeks of infantry training prior to being posted to our battalions, in my case 1 Para. There were a number of exercises, including two descents on to Hankley Common. Days and days were also spent on the ranges. On completing recruit training, we were each marched in for an interview with the Depot OC. I think his name was Major Maurice Tugwell. I remember the occasion well, and in particular the advice imparted. His brief words went something like this: "You've done well to get through, Rowlands, and merit congratulations. But looking at your reports there is nothing particularly remarkable about you. You have not scored above average in anything. The best thing you can do is concentrate on being reliable. As you go through life you will find much unreliability. But if you can build a personal reputation for reliability, you will get on in 1 Para, and in later life." I reckon that to have been a very profound statement. Reliability is indeed a scarce commodity. But I have generally found Paras and ex-Paras to be true to their word – they will be where they say will be, on time and with the right kit. And so my years in 1 Para ensued. At the end of the three years for which I had enlisted, I received no divine inspiration on what career I wanted to follow longer-term. At the three-year stage life was pretty good. I had a couple of stripes, and was half way through a twelve month tour in the Persian Gulf. So it made good sense to simply sign on for a further term. The next three years proved rather less peaceful. But this short piece is about recruitment and training – and that's another story.

—MR

12
CYPRUS – NEW YEARS DAY 1964

On New Year's Day 1964 we arrived at Nicosia Airport as members of a British Parachute Battalion Group with the intention of stopping the Greek Cypriots from killing off all the Turkish Cypriots in Cyprus, particularly in Nicosia. The President of Cyprus was Archbishop Makarios, a Greek Cypriot who had made it quite clear that he had no love for his Turkish Cypriot compatriots or for the British. We would, a few months later become the first ever British Parachute troops – indeed the first ever British Troops of any Corps or Regiment – to take off our red berets to wear the blue United Nations headgear! Replacing our red berets with the United Nations headgear was not, to say the least, a popular decision. Therefore to keep us happy we were allowed to wear a maroon patch behind the United Nations cap badge. Again this was unprecedented. We all knew the eyes of the World were on us and that we were to show the utmost restraint and show no bias to either side. This, of course, would not be easy as for years the Greek Cypriots had been waging a war against British troops! However, we had been briefed in Aldershot and because we were soldiers had obviously accepted the situation. As a show of force and to demonstrate our neutrality, we paraded as a Battalion Group in full kit on Day One on the airfield. The Regimental Sergeant Major, a veteran of World War II, Jerusalem, the Radfan etc, strode out in front of us and in his long remembered speech began with the words "Now there is this swine called Mac Hairy Arse!"... We ceased to be neutral instantly (in mind if nothing else!)

—JT

13
THE DAY CHARLIE WATTS THREW A WOBBLER

Eddie Jackson was the sort of person that legends grew around. He did have his fair share of idiosyncrasies, claiming to be descended from both Stonewall Jackson and Oliver Cromwell – but it was his self-effacement which endeared him to the memory, not so much his actions, as his bewilderment at others reactions, his calm acceptance of being "the sort that things happen to". Another characteristic was his inability to stifle his more provocative utterances. As he confided to me once "It's as though somebody else is talking, It just sounds like me but of course, as Scouse Morrow would have it, 'I mean, who else sounds like him', besides, it sounds like bullshit but you can't be sure can you, not with Eddie". The worthy Liverpudlian had a point, as some of the more bizarre stories about Eddie were sometimes confirmed by unimpeachable sources. For example the stalwart figure of Sergeant Don Newlands, all twelve calvinistic stone of him, attesting to the day that Charlie Watts threw a wobbler. Captain Watts, Officer Commanding Stores Section, (RAOC) attached to sixteen Parachute Workshops, (REME), was a thin, bird like man, unprepossessing in appearance but not a bad sort. He was known affectionately as Charlie because he had the same surname as the drummer of the Rolling Stones. There was an actress at the time called Queenie Watts but you couldn't call Captain Watts, Queenie. Besides that was the Sergeant Major's nickname. But that's another story. Captain Carswell, the Workshops Officer realized the necessity of a good Stores Section and so Charlie was accepted by the other Officers of the Workshops as, if not an equal, an integral part of the functioning of the Unit. And to his credit, he was a good O.C. If the O.C. of a Stores section was to be his lot in life so be it, but it would be the best Stores Section in the British Army worthy of its airborne affiliation. He would buff and pamper it jealously, making sure that each part of it worked as efficiently as possible.

That was how it began. When Eddie joined the Stores Section he was given the position of indent clerk, this consisted of maintaining the Indent Register (I hope this doesn't contravene the Official Secrets Act) which was a Register of Indents or Demands for Spare Parts, where the Indent number of the item ordered was entered on the left followed by the Part Number, date, etc. etc. So there Eddie was, probably reflecting that this was not his image of being a Paratrooper, or calculating the return on a horse coming in second at 12 to 1, when he made an entry for one particular indent. Where the previous entry was 01299 the next one should have been 01300 where Eddie (perhaps distracted by his calculations) put 01290, and therefore the numbers between 01299 and 01290 were duplicated.

Things came to a boil (almost literally) when the receipt of a gearbox for a Landrover was checked against the Indent Register where apparently a pair of wiper blades had been ordered, and Eddie's successor as Indent Clerk, one Lance Corporal Ray Doran successfully proved (without being asked to) that he was nowhere within thirty miles of the Indent Register when the offending entry was made. So the blame trickled inexorably down to Eddie who, in response to a hushed summons presented himself, or was escorted by Sergeant Don Newlands, to the O.C.s office.

There was Charlie Watts, all nine forbidding stone of him and before him was, the Indent Register. Striving to keep his tone neutral, as befitting a holder of the Queen's Commission (RAOC) he opened the proceedings. "Jackson," he said, "do you know anything about this?"

He touched the book with the tip of his pencil.

"The Indent Register, sir? It's—"

"This!" The pencil was jabbed at the entry as though Charlie was trying to stab a cobra.

"That's the Indent number column, sir."

"Could you read it for me?"

Eddie craned his neck with some difficulty as he was standing loosely to attention.

"01290, sir."

"And this?" The pencil moved up ten lines.

"That's – 01290, sir."

"So," Charlie steepled his fingers, "we have from 01290 to 01299 duplicated, what have you to say to that?" Charlie glanced briefly at his audience and Don Newlands while maintaining the posture of attention, managed a pained expression.

"Could we just add an A to the bottom row sir making it 01290 stroke A and—"

"The point is, all this would have been unnecessary if it had been done correctly to start with but we'll get back to that. When were you Indent Clerk?"

"From when I joined the Unit sir – September last year to March about—" He got no further as Charlie Watts, using the tips of his fingers to reverse the position of the book, "Would you read the date next to the entry?"

"February the fourteenth sir, Saint Valentines—"

"So it was while you were Indent Clerk?"

"Yes sir."

"And during this time you've not been away from the Unit – Christian Leadership Courses – Trade upgrading, hm?"

"No, sir."

"You weren't off sick, no broken legs – blackouts."

"No, sir."

"So would it be safe to assume that you are responsible for – this," again the tip of the pencil barely touched the offending entry.

"It's probably me sir," Eddie conceded magnanimously, "but it's only ten entries – lucky we caught it in time." "Lucky?" Charlie Watts closed the book as though the very sight was painful to him and stared down at it while continuing with awesome control. "I think you'd better leave before I lose my temper."

Apparently he meant both of them and Don Newlands did a smart right turn and left the office. He was halfway across the floor, and was about to admonish Eddie as to how lightly he'd got off when he realized he was alone. After looking around he uncertainly made his way back to Captain Watts's office and had reached the open door in time to witness what happened next. Charlie Watts had brought himself to open the book and was amending the duplicated Indent numbers with an A when he realised he was not alone, Eddie had not moved. "You–may–leave."

"Must I sir? – only – I've never seen an Officer lose his temper." CHARLIE WATTS LEVITATED. The pent up passion finally became too much for his scrawny breast and he actually rose inches from the chair

His normally pale face was the colour of candle wax and strangled gasps came from his mouth. "GET – GET HIM —" He pointed a shaking finger at Eddie who was saved from further contemplation of this awesome spectacle by Don Newlands grabbing the back of his neck and dragging him out of the office. It was not until they had reached the area where Don had lost Eddie when he was released. "Not got much of a sense of humour has he."

"Follow me!"

And that was it until they reached the Sergeant Major's Office and Don had knocked on the door.

"The Sergeant Major's got even less of one so–"

"Enter"

"–Leave the talking to me." Sergeant Major Plummer kept them waiting the prescribed thirty seconds before he looked up from the Guard Roster. "Good morning Sergeant Newlands and–" his gaze shifted to Eddie, "what have we here?"

"Jackson sir," Don Newlands supplied. "Volunteering for cookhouse fatigues."

"Splendid" Jerry Plummer pulled a form towards him, "J-A-C-K-S-O-N?"

"Yes, sir"

"Right, thank you Sergeant Newlands, and do you know when I can expect the other six names?"

"Him sir, he's yours all week, compliments of Captain Watts."

"Oh I see well – Jackson – you will report to Sergeant Reynolds at Arnhem Cookhouse, at 0800 hours Monday – Fatigue – Dress – and you will be in under his charge until he dismisses you on Sunday evening – clear?"

"Yes, sir."

"Good – not the pleasantest of tasks but these things have to be done."

"I'll go wherever my duty takes me, sir."

"Quite! Thank you Sergeant Newlands, my compliments to Captain Watts." Outside Don Newlands turned to Eddie, "Don't forget to check on Part 1 Orders each day to see if you're on Guard and obviously on Friday night to see if you're on duty over the weekend and when you've finished on Sunday check with – any NCOs' living in?"

"Corporal Macullum."

"Right check with Andy, I'll tell him."

"Tell him what?"

Without breaking step Don Newlands replied, "If it's safe for you to come back to the unit"

Eddie finished his week of purgatory in the kitchen more or less to Sergeant Reynolds satisfaction and was relieved to learn from Andy Macallum that it was safe to venture back to the Store's Section with the admonition, "– Better give Charlie a wide berth to be on the safe side.

After that there was an exercise in Yorkshire, Brigade weapons week (where the Workshops team finished embarrassingly higher than many Regimental teams) and various football games. The day that Charlie Watts threw a wobbler was safely ensconced in legends of the Unit, and Eddie had even given up going through the workshops to avoid passing Charlie's office when the summons came. The welcome was ominously cordial,

"Jackson! Come in, take the weight off" – he was waved to a chair. What looked suspiciously like his personal file was on the desk.

"Know anything about Libya?"

"Libya? North Africa Sir, next to Egypt."

"That's the one – fancy a couple of weeks there? The Brigade has been asked to supply bodies, a few from each Unit, for parachute trials on a new aircraft, the Andover – very short take-off and landing, useful in jungle airstrips," he lowered his voice, "Vietnam," he pulled Eddie's file towards him, "your Jabs are up to date – passport all right – run by MOD so discipline will not be too bad, you've been an Eight Jump Wonder long enough - time to get your knees brown, what do you think?"

"Great, sir."

"Good man – Corporal Thompson in the Orderly Room will send the details as soon as he gets them – all right?"

"Yes Sir."

"Good - thank you Jackson."

Eddie turned to leave. "There is one more thing."

"Sir?"

"You might as well have a shufti at this before you go—" Charlie pulled a foolscap sheet from the file and offered to Eddie, "it's your fitness report, sign it at the bottom, you're signing to say that you've read it, not that you agree with it necessarily, take your time, ask any questions you want."

Eddie read.

'Private Jackson was inclined to be impulsive, he would tend to rush in to things without fully understanding what he was doing and without fully appreciating the consequences. Nevertheless, he has matured into a well turned out; loyal efficient member of the Unit and his dry sense of humour is an asset.'

"Any questions?"

"Well, sir – impulsive?"

"Yes, Jackson," Charlie closed his eyes painfully, "the Indent Register."

"Oh yes, Sir, your point is well taken and thank you for the rest of it."

"Not at all," Charlie opened his eyes, "you've heard about the three ways, the right way the wrong way and the Army way?"

"Yes, sir."

"Well! The Army way is nearly always the right way and the few times it isn't, it's still the Army way. Anyway, shall we agree that three ways is enough, we don't need a fourth?"

"Yes, sir?"

"Good man; off you go."

So he had a sense of humour after all!

—SEC

14
WHEN "HAPPY HOUR" CAME EARLY

The old man was bemused, if not bewildered. I was trying to give him a few lines of very basic Arabic that I had been taught in the Education Centre in Aldershot, (when I was listening). I would imagine he was more interested in the weapon I was carrying, and those of the patrol around me. He was something of a watchman, for the car dump, in which we found him. There was a strong suspicion that one of the local terrorist gangs was using the dump, as a firing point, to have a go at us at, "Happy Hour", (Happy Hour was when darkness fell, quickly, in Aden. That was the opportunity for all happy little terrorists to try and blast us into the other world, and we, of course, would return the compliment.). I was interrogating this chap. My brain was telling me that I knew what I wanted to ask him, but there was no guarantee my words in Arabic bore any relation to the subject. Anyway, eventually, I briefed our Platoon Commander that either he knew nothing, or was far too scared of the possible consequences to bubble the local Mafia to us. We were slowly patrolling our way back towards our OP, when suddenly there was a line of little spurts of sand in front of me; then I heard the shots. As I had been last man to leave the car dump, I was now last in the patrol. The other lads had all sprinted forward and got down behind a massive oil pipe, of which there many in the Middle East, (all smelly), and returned the fire. The nearest cover to me was a solitary Arab toilet block. I sprinted to it and launched myself through the doorway. My DMS Boots landed on a wet and shiny marble floor. There followed the most impressive of back flips, a splitting of my denims, and a final landing place on top of where Arabs deposit their daily woopsies! Not too glorious actually.

I am not likely to forget the next event. Whoever, or how many, of the local happy little terrorists, had decided to try and shoot us up the jacksie, they had not thought out the situation too well. Our initial return of fire was about nine automatic weapons from the patrol members, all at the same time. This was shortly joined by the GPMG on the roof of our OP, putting down a heavy hail of fire. Within minutes a Ferret Armoured Car came hurtling round the corner, and opened up fire with his .5 Browning Heavy Machine Gun. The fire was so intense that local huts, (they were called "Kutchi" Huts by us, due to the fact that were assembled from cardboard boxes), were soon in flames. In the middle of this entire inferno, I spotted an Arab woman, in long black robes, just simply walking straight through this maelstrom of fire, and out the other end untouched. I am sure if she had stopped, or tried to run, she would probably have been cut down. Amazing, I have to say, in my up until then three years service, this was the first time I had actually been involved in a fire-fight in broad daylight. As I said, most "Happy Hours" are in the dark.

—AM

15
A "FIREY" DAY IN JUNE

The following words are my recollections of an event some forty-seven years ago; 1st of June 1967, in Aden. It is relatively important to accept that, at that time, I was a twenty-one year-old very simple Private soldier, whose life was actually quite simple – just do as I was told… or else. I had not even completed three years service by then, so my military experience and understanding was pretty limited. Now, in hindsight, having served for over thirty-five years, with a bit more knowledge and experience, would I have reacted any differently? There would most certainly have been a world of difference between the then, pretty fit, twenty-one year-old Private and a half deaf, sciatic retired Major slipping into senility. However, this is more concerning what I can recall about that particular day, which, for those of us involved, we will never forget whilst we draw breath, nor should we. We were 1st Battalion the Parachute Regiment (1 PARA) and we were based in Radfan Camp, Aden. This was a tented camp, probably about halfway between Aden and the Arab settlement of Sheikh Othman, and opposite both the RAF Airfield at Khormaksar and near to the Arab Police Lines. I believe we were positioned there because our area of operation was predominantly Sheikh Othman. We took over both the Camp and responsibility for Sheikh Othman in early 1967. Our Company flew out from Gatwick sometime in May 1967. We had been in Aden before, in 1965. We had been based in Bahrain, with responsibility for the Radfan/Yemen Border area, north of Aden. In September 1965, our Company were due to do our second six week tour in the Radfan, but we were diverted at RAF Khormaksar, because the troubles and tension in Aden itself had increased. So we spent a rather pleasant and easy six weeks in Singapore Lines. The trouble at that time was crowd control and the odd flashpoint, so we were pretty safe to travel around the area as we wished. It was a different scenario when we came back in '67.

Remembering that I was but a simple Private soldier, of the simplest type, my understanding of why we were there in '67, was, at best, pretty limited. I do recall subscribing to the argument that we should not be there. It should be our sister battalion, 3 PARA. This conclusion was pure NAAFI logic. We all knew that each of our Battalions did one year, in turn, in Bahrain, (and Aden). We had done '65 to '66, and were replaced by 2 PARA for '66 to early '67. Therefore, it must have been the turn of 3 PARA? Ours not to understand that, Bahrain, as a Tour, was probably finished by then, or indeed the logic of the Army Board on current operational commitments. All we knew and muttered about was that 3 PARA were on holiday in Malta or British Guiana or somewhere, whilst we patrolled the smelly back streets of Aden. I was probably more interested in how cheap the beer was in the NAAFI, even if it was warm. Also, I would be constantly whingeing about why we had to go on patrols, when we should really be down on the lovely beach at the Mermaid Club in Steamer Point. I recall that there were three factions, or terrorist groups, fighting amongst themselves for power in Aden, and, of course fighting against us. NLF, (National Liberation Front), seemed to be the strongest of the three. The other two were FLOSY, (Front for the Liberation of Southern Yemen), and PORF, (cannot recall who they represented, but they did have a lot of Somalis amongst them). All of them, of course, were well supported by our old friends the Soviets, all channelled through Egypt. It was of no great surprise that most of the weapons we were to recover from local Arabs were Russian Kalashnikovs. Mr Nasser was still holding the seat in Egypt at that time. They hated us, almost as badly as they hated the Jews. I do recall that in that year, the Egyptians had an away war against the Israelis and lost, again. The background to the 1st of June '67 appeared to be that the three rival groups had called some sort of truce between themselves for that particular day, and were calling for a general strike in Sheikh Othman. They had done that around Easter '67 and had attacked the Battalion in that area; to the extent that I was told the British Troops had to withdraw. It appeared they did not want the Red Beret types to settle and we were to get the same treatment on 1st of June. However, this time, our people knew about it beforehand. I knew there was something different going on because, in the evening of 31st May we were all briefed about an early-morning deployment, told to get all our kit ready, ammunition, etc, and get to bed fully dressed! Sure enough at 02:00 hours we were all roused and told to get on the waiting trucks. We disembarked just outside Sheikers, and patrolled down both sides of the road into the settlement. We stopped at OP, (Observation Post), eight, which was on the bottom edge of Sheikh Othman, beside the road that ran down to Mansoora Prison. Rooftop Sentries and Arcs of Fire were sorted out pretty quickly, (because the whole Company was deployed on OPs throughout the village, arcs of fire were most important, to stop you shooting each other!), and for the rest of us to try and catch some sleep. My memory is absolutely crystal clear on our wakeup call! At 05:20 hours a Blindicide Rocket came through our room window. What clearly saved us from serious damage were the wooden shutters on the outside of the window, which took the impact and most of the explosion. I do remember we were staggering around in a grey cloud of smoke and dust, temporarily deafened by the blast wave. By this time it was daylight, and time for the locals to get going at us. I was told later that, at any one time, all twelve of our OPs were coming under fire, from up to five different firing points each.

That means up to sixty different fire points giving us grief all at the same time; an awful lot of angry Arabs. Our little Section was about nine strong. We were well led by a true character, Corporal Bob. I think the rest of us were all, "Toms", (Privates), Dave, Spick, Noddy, two lads from 216 Para Sig Sqn, Jimmy and Mick, Piggy, Jumbo and me. On this particular day we were reinforced by more of our Platoon under Cpl Tom M, (a real cool character), and all under command of Lt Dick and Sgt Barry.

Although there was an awful lot of firing going on and massive radio chatter, it does not take long to get into a routine. There would probably be two or even three of us on the roof at any one time, with an NCO keeping his eye on what we were shooting at. Everyone else would be kipping or eating downstairs. Apart from Tom. He had identified a possible sniper. It seemed to me that Tom kept the shot for shot going with this particular individual for many long hours. Eventually Tom fired a shot, but remained in the aim for a few seconds, and then fired again. It worked, as we saw a weapon fall out of a window, but no body. A cool customer. I cannot recall the number of another of our OPs, but I do remember we could look down on their roof from our position. We were concerned about this because there were other taller buildings in the area. We were also aware that there was an East German Mercenary sniper operating in that area. Sadly, our concerns were justified. About mid-morning that particular OP came under really heavy fire from many positions. This is normally the cover for a sniper to do his work. The number two on the Machine Group was reinforcement from C Company by the name of Pte Carver. I am told he was just checking his arc of fire, had pushed the GPMG, (General Purpose Machine Gun), to one side so he could get a better view. When his face appeared in the slit, the sniper put a round straight through his nose. Tom's younger brother, Charlie, was on that roof and handled the situation very well; calmed them all down and carrying young Carver's body cleared them down to safety. We were sent out later, in a strong patrol, to help the vehicles recover the Section and the body. It was just a bit hairy! I remember standing on the corner, as Lead Scout, watching these little spurts of sand stitching up the road beside me, before I heard the shots. It missed me, Noddy behind me, and hit Vic in the foot, (a Blighty wound – but he was back with us by September). We were all desperately looking for cover. I was facing a blue wooden door; I had seen all the good cowboy films. So I launched myself in midair, feet first at the door…bounced-off and sat on my arse in the sand! Lt Dick then proceeded to bollock me, and told me to stop f**king about and get into cover! Lovely. Mick and I found an old tree in the roadway and got down on either side of it to fire back. Not ideal, but at least we were down and off our feet. Shortly, a trusty old Ferret armoured car came round the corner, and proceeded to give all the windows and roofs a good old hosing down with his Browning Machine Gun. Gave us the break, space and time we needed, to get the job done, and get out of that area. During all this time, Tom, was sheltering in a shop doorway, sipping a bottle of iced coke…. Calm man. Shortly after that, one of the lads, "Black Al", (Al who looked more Pakistani than a Pakistani, but was a London boy), had an amazing escape. Al was having a breather just outside OP 4. OP 4 was the main Police Station in Sheikh Othman. He was taking cover behind a large stack of crates of empty Coca-Cola bottles. A grenade was thrown and landed on top of the crates. The explosion blew up and out from the crates, and actually went over the top of Al. He escaped with a few scratches from flying glass, mumbling about sod this for a joke! Back at our OP, a welcome sight just after noon was Middy. Middy was our CSM, (Company Sergeant Major – Warrant Officer Class 2 – and he who must be obeyed). Middy had earned his respect over the years in various far flung operations worldwide, and being a sound Liverpool Lad, was not one known to back down from anything or anybody. He actually cared very deeply for his Company, and we were all the better for that, even if we did not know or think so at the time. Middy had arrived in a "Pig", (large armoured personnel carrier), and brought along a very necessary ammunition resupply and containers of "All-In Airborne Stew". Both were most gratefully received. Middy would never show concerns or worry about the situation we had found ourselves in. That is what we were trained for and supposed to do well. He would make light of it by a mild rebuke about your beret not being straight or your belt order not done-up properly. He was a good man to have around because his very presence brought a sense of calmness and normality to whatever was happening around you. He was to be injured and casevacced later in the year, as the result of a rocket blast, which was of great concern to us. However, they could not keep him in UK for long, and he was back getting back in amongst us with his sharp Scouse tongue.

Another of our OPs was on top of the Bank. The Bank faced the main Mosque.

Although we were not allowed under any circumstances to enter the Mosque, that did not stop the occupants from using it as one of their fire bases; funny the way religion does not necessarily work both ways at times. Their fire from the Mosque was becoming pretty heavy, constant and just getting too accurate. Hoss and Frank set up their GPMG on the roof of the Bank, facing the mosque. Frank then clipped about five two hundred round belts together, and as Hoss put concentrated fire through the Mosque main door and windows, Frank kept the ammunition free and clean. Although we could not enter the building, nobody said we could not fire back! By the time the thousand rounds had gone home, the gun barrel was overheating, and the Mosque doors were well ablaze. There was no more firing from the building. Times like these always need the humorous content. Ours was our Company Clerk, Cpl Dickey. Dickey was another good lad, and a bit of an old sweat. A little Cockney with a lively sense of humour, who could talk the hinges of a barn door. Unfortunately, with his poor eyesight, he could not hit said barn door, even if he had been holding it in his other hand! Later in the day, Dickey was also doing a stag, (tour of sentry duty), on the roof of the Bank. He spotted a guy with a rifle running across an alleyway, and engaged him with his SMG, (Sub Machine Gun). The "Guy" was actually a member of the KOSBR who were patrolling just on the edge of Sheikers. Fortunately for him, it was Dickey who was blasting away at him, and unless he was really unlucky, he was in no real danger. Although I suspect his heart beat increased just a bit and his speed across the alley! Others tried to point out to Dickey that the Guy was wearing KDs, (sand coloured uniform), and a belt order, but no one could convince our Dickey that he must have been nothing less than a KOSBR Terrorist! Incidents like the above were pretty much the pattern of the day, and no doubt why we will not forget it in our time. It started to tail off after last light, about the back of seven in the evening. They could not see us and we could not see them, so nothing to shoot at. The "Pigs" came back about ten o'clock that night, and we all scampered out of our bolt holes, for the drive back to camp. Except Kip! I still cannot understand what went wrong or how he was missed on the transport. The commonly accepted explanation was that, Kip was known to be a deep sleeper, as in bordering on unconsciousness. When we exfiltrated from the OP clearly there were no lights or sound to give away our actions, complete darkness and silence. Kip just simply kept on kipping! When he did wake-up, around first light, he realised, quickly, that he was on his own. He hightailed it, very quickly out of there, and across the open ground towards the Manoora OP, in the opposite direction from Sheikh Othman. A bleary eyed sentry on that OP spotted a guy, carrying a rifle, legging it across the open ground towards them. Right then, he must have thought, as he got himself into a good firing position, and started to take a careful aim on his "target". Fortunately, he was checked by his NCO, who had also spotted the target, and when closing in on him with his binoculars, noted that the man was wearing jungle greens, a belt order, and carrying an SLR. He was also lumbering along like a demented prop forward, which Kip, a good big Lancashire Lad, happened to be. Kip was back in our Lines by breakfast on 2nd June, much to our relief and no doubt his! I am sure there would have been many questions asked in the Company Headquarters and or the Sergeant's Mess, but as it came to a happy ending, it was swiftly passed over. When we got back to camp, about midnight, it was the normal routine of returning cleaned weapons and ammunition to the armoury. I have no memories of any back slapping or jumping about by the boys. It had been a very long day and some scoff and a good sleep were the top priorities. I do admit that I was having the odd dose of the shakes when I was cleaning my weapon, and if that was what they call post reaction, then so be it. I think because everyone was simply being their normal self, and just wanted their bed, there was no sense or feeling of a, "big deal". I think we felt that was for those that wanted to be that way, not for our Teams. After a very good sleep, we were up in the morning for Middy's Muster Parade, and then he had us off to the bottom of the camp… To fill the never ending sand bags… No change there then.

    Just before Lunch, the Commanding Officer, Lt Col Mike came to talk to us. He told us that the 1st of June had been the most significant day of the Tour so far, and we had given a first rate and professional account of ourselves, with a "Well Done", and, "Thank You", even. Better news was to follow from Middy, who told us all to get off sharply, get our towels and trunks, and get on the trucks. Rest of the day off down at yonder Mermaid Club… Good oh! The result of June the First was very evident from then onwards in Sheikh Othman. It went fairly quiet and terrorist incidents dropped off significantly. I believe they stood up and had a go at us, and failed. They went back to shooting each other amongst their three different groups. Activities against British soldiers moved to other areas of Aden. Not so good for the other Regiments but a bit of a break for us. Apart from young Carver, we lost two other lads on that tour. I think they were Ptes Quinn and MacIntosh both very young. I recall that we had a Drum Head Service on the Camp Football Pitch for young MacIntosh. I vividly remember thinking to myself, what if this was not for young MacIntosh, but for young MacLaren. I quickly shook myself away from that train of thought, because we all knew, it was not going to happen to you, was it? You had to think that way. In no way was it bravado of any kind, just sheer common sense and survival. My constant sad memory is that those three young lads never got back to these shores. It did not happen in those days. They are at rest In Silent Valley Military Cemetery outside Little Aden, a far cry from the pubs of Aldershot. Our Company lost no one. Our Officer Commanding, Major Geoff, always appeared to be totally unforgiving towards us in his attitude. Ably supported by his CSM, Middy. There seemed to be no let-up, or words of well done, just constant operations, training and daily discipline.

The reason for all of that became clear to us the day before we left Aden. The OC addressed us all in the Camp Briefing Room. All he said was that we all came out on the same aircraft, and we will all return home together, and he had done his job. I think then we all felt so humble and just a wee bit proud. Although I was clearly delighted to leave Aden at the end of November 1967, (and who would not be), today I have mixed feelings about that. I learned later that the UK Government had actually recognised the NLF as the ruling Party in Aden, and I had heard that they gave them some thirteen million pounds to help them on their way? What was all that about? If this is true, I for one am not happy about that. I can just imagine what that decision would have meant to all of the families of those young men who remain in Silent Valley. I think we could, and should have had at least a service or parade in Silent Valley, to say our farewells, before we returned home. That said, the euphoria of our departure was brilliant. On 28th November we formed up in our Companies and in our best KDs. The CO led us out of Radfan Camp, Band playing, Colours flying. As we passed the loading/unloading bays, and within eyesight of the Arab Police Barracks, (who had mutinied in July and killed several British soldiers), we loaded and cocked our weapons in a brisk military manner! Have a last go if you want Matey?? We then crossed over onto RAF Khormaksar, and the departing Aden Brigade Commander took the salute on our March Past on the runway. We then nestled in the back of the Hangars until just before midnight. A fleet of what were brand new aircraft to us, Hercules C130s, landed and taxied up the runways, with tailgates down. We ran out in Company Groups, straight into the rear of the rolling Hercules, and then off! Something like the future raid on Entebbe in reverse.

We flew to Bahrain, but stopping at Salalah and Sharjah en route. On arrival at RAF Muharraq on Bahrain, the Royal Army

Ordnance Corps had set-up a tented city for us. In one tent, we handed in our weapons and ammunition, in another our webbing. We were then reunited with our suitcases. After changing into our civilian clothes, we then took our KDs to a central area, where they were promptly burned. After a few hours hanging about, we were bussed out to our waiting Britannia aircraft, and off back to Gatwick. Over the years, we have had a few 1st of June reunions. Sadly though, none of us have retained our youth, and the grim reaper has taken quite a few of our number. Those who remain will no doubt still have their own strong memories. Once all the euphoria had worn off, and many years later, I had to question myself, why did we leave in such a manner? We were not exactly being hounded down the runway by terrorists. The fighting was over. We had done the job that was given to us. The stuffing had been knocked out of the terrorists and Aden was a much more peaceful place. I am sure that those in higher circles than I ever got anywhere near will have taken logical counsel, and decided a silent and secretive withdrawal was by far the best and safest option. Even so, I find that a bitter pill to swallow, and I for one could never agree to that, or the recognition of the NLF…our enemy. It is probably fitting, at this juncture, that I do not claim, "Author's Licence".

My ramblings may not be completely accurate, and indeed I would be most surprised if they were. As stated, I was a simple soldier in a section of nine. Our section, at that time, in that place, was our world. Our section Corporal was our God. Simply, you were in our section, or you did not really matter. It was a good system, and I do hope and suspect that it will not be so different in today's infantry. It worked well. However, where I have recalled actions that I saw or was involved in… They happened.

But as I repeated at the beginning of this tome, my words are about that day in Aden. In summary, I am left with two outstanding memories of 1st June 1967. In a non-perverse way, I am so glad that I was there, and allowed to play my small role in that memorable day. I am so humble and proud that I was given the opportunity to serve with such professional soldiers, who took that day in their stride, much the same as any other task, or any other day, given to them. It is so refreshing, and indeed humbling, that our Boys and Girls in present day Afghanistan seem to take each event and day, in their stride. God bless them and look after them.
Utrinque Paratus

—AM

16
PULLING THE FLAG DOWN

Ray Doran and I were the last permanent residents to leave Radfan Camp in Aden at the end of the occupancy by the 1st Battalion the Parachute Regiment. It wasn't planned that way, in fact we had our freshly laundered KDs hanging in the back of the Landrover preparatory to joining the rest of the battalion who were at that moment marching six abreast down the main runway of RAF Khormaksar (much to the consternation of the worthy RAF types in the control tower) and I could regale you with images of pulling the flag down and watching the sun set on the empire as it sank beneath the Indian Ocean, but the fact was that Ray had commandeered a Landrover and the services of yours truly to conduct a little last minute business concerning some risqué films.

The thinking was, the aircraft which were supposed to whisk us away to hearth and home were within range of Blindicides, a crude rocket launcher made out of drainpipes and used to great effect by the gentlemen of the NLF and the more grandiosely titled FLOSY, both of whom would welcome the chance of taking one last cheap shot at the 1st. Battalion the Parachute Regiment. 45 Royal Marine Commando, did not suffer from this anxiety, apart from the fact that their ships were anchored well out of range of the blindicides the commandos were too well bred to garner such ill intent and so it was decided that the 45 Commando should throw a defensive perimeter round Radfan Camp and Khormaksar airfield while we took our not too tearful farewell. So there we were, with the films (this was 1967, before the advent of video cassettes) snugly in Ray's flight bag, as we slowed to a halt at the Marine check point on the main gate.

"Let me do the talking," Ray muttered (I had no intention of doing anything else) as a newly washed and pressed Marine Lieutenant approached the vehicle.

"So you're part of the dreaded 1 Para"

"Just trying to do our bit Sir" Ray threw him one up, "–same as you"

'Yes" He drawled as he returned Ray's salute, "–hope it's not too much of an indignity, The Royal Marines covering your, ahem, withdrawal,"

"Couldn't wish for more capable hands to leave the Empire in sir" Ray waited until the barrier was raised and we were almost out of earshot before he added,

"As long as I get my oats before Christmas the f******' 11th Hampshire Girl Guides can cover my ahem f******' withdrawal"

And with this pleasantry we turned our backs on the British presence East of Suez.

—SEC

17
DOBBIE'S BUCKSHEE STEAK AND KIDNEY PIE

I have read often about bullying in the Armed Services but I can honestly say that during all my Army Service I never came across any. There were instances of extreme cruelty, for instance – Paras Kill Thirteen, they call it Bloody Sunday what do we call it? – A good start -- but the soldier who coined this masterpiece was probably one who had tried to stop the locals urinating on the body of Sergeant Showell who had been killed by an IRA bomb while shepherding the inhabitants of a youth club to safety.

There were also moments of unexpected compassion and one of them concerned Dobbie and a Steak and Kidney Pie. Dobbie was the Second-in-Command of the unit. He had originally possessed a double barrelled name of which Dobson was the first half but in thirty odd years of Army service he had lost the second half, and the remainder had been personalised to Dobbie. No one knew why he survived in the British army let alone an airborne unit. Popular myth had it that he had performed some act of service for the Brigadier when both were prisoners of the Chinese during the Korean conflict. Apparently during the march to their prison camp if anyone dropped out they were left to freeze to death and Dobbie being in slightly better condition than the Brigadier, supported him enough to prevent him being left to his fate, or as in the less charitable interpretation, "He carry's the Brigadier half a mile so we have to carry him the rest of his life." That was the legend and nobody seemed inclined to ask Dobbie as he ambled on his way smiling at nothing in particular and saluting everyone in sight, finding time along the way to acquire, or be acquired by, a wife, the formidable Mrs Dobbie, who, in the best traditions of an Army wife (officer type) when she was not intimidating the hapless Dobbie would sally forth dispensing unsolicited advice to the less fortunate.

Whenever Mrs Dobbie was out of town on her good works or she wanted Dobbie out from under her feet she would allow him the sum of One Shilling for a NAAFI steak and kidney pie (although it didn't contain anything remotely resembling a kidney and the nearest the "steak" got to a cow was the NAAFI manageress) for his lunch. The actual purchase of this delicacy was entrusted to Kenny Bartlet, because his was the only name Dobbie could remember on a regular basis.

At the time in question Mrs Dobbie's good works had called her away for a week and so Dobbie's stipend had been raised to the princely sum of five shillings. Unfortunately on the Monday morning that began Mrs Dobbie's absence the price of the Steak and Kidney pies was raised to One Shilling and Threepence which meant that the sum nestling in Dobbie's pocket was sufficient for only four days sustenance and as the Friday approached everyone was anticipating how Kenny would handle it, for Dobbie's financial arrangements were well known in the unit.

Came the day and Kenny was equal to it, instead of visiting the Orderly Room en route to the NAAFI he went immediately there and ordered the meat pie as usual. NAAFI break over Kenny presented his good self at the Orderly Room, together with one NAAFI Steak and Kidney Pie. It seemed that everyone in the unit had pressing business in or near the Orderly Room that morning and so Dobbie's futile fumbling were well witnessed until they were brought to a merciful end by Kenny's well rehearsed disclosure, "It's all right sir, that one's buckshee."

"Buckshee Baker? er Barnet er Bartlet – Buckshee?"

"Yes sir, an American idea, you buy four in a week and the Fifth one's buckshee," Dobbie's thanks were waved away and Kenny offered a silent prayer that Mrs Dobbie would find more to occupy herself nearer home in the future.

N.B. NAAFI Naval Army and Air force Institution. Or in the less sparing language of the junior ranks; No Ambition and F*** All Interest.

—SEC

18
THE HANDOVER PARADE

In the late sixties HQ Allied Forces Central Europe (AFCENT) was kicked out of France by General De Gaulle and the command passed from a French General to a German who had served with distinction during the Second World War, but who had not been a Nazi. He had therefore been accepted into the new Bundeswehr on formation in 1957. Each of the seven nations comprising the Headquarters had to produce a 50 man guard to take part in the handover parade and ours was found from the HQ staff, a mixture of RAOC clerks, RASC drivers and RE draughtsmen. It was commanded by a young RA Captain. Most of us were in our early twenties but the oldest man on parade was a driver who had served in North Africa during the war. He was reputed to have risen all the way up to RSM and then back down all the way to private soldier in his long career mainly due to a strong affinity to beer. The rehearsals went well and the British guard was acknowledged by all as the smartest cohort on parade. When the two Generals emerged from the main building and began to inspect the troops the young Captain to our front began to quiver ever so slightly. He had obviously just had the same thought as the rest of us. If you are a General inspecting a row of soldiers and one of them has a chest full of medals... Who are you going to talk to? With a charming smile he approached our guard and sure as eggs headed for the ancient staff car driver. "How haff you earned all zese medals?" said he. "Killin' Germans, Sir!" was the answer! The sight of fifty men internalising their hysterics was a joy to behold!

—CW

19
16 PARA HY DROP COMPANY RAOC WATCHFIELD

Two amusing incidents I remember from my early days in 16 Para Hy Drop were: ONE. A young soldier called Paddy (he was Irish!) had broken a leg playing rugby and just when it got to the healing stage, six weeks or so, he went out on his motorbike, had an argument with a rather large tree and broke his leg AGAIN. When he was declared fit after this, another six weeks or so – he was detailed for a parachute training exercise on Watchfield DZ, then the home of 16 Para Hy Drop. It was a night jump and the large hangars around the DZ were grass covered. Paddy landed safely, rolled up his parachute, put it on his back and began walking off the DZ. Little did he know that he had landed on the top of one of the grass covered hangars. He walked off THE END of one of them, about a 20ft drop and guess what...? YES, he broke his leg again!

TWO. The married quarters at Watchfield were very close to the DZ. One very windy day the unit were doing a parachute training exercise on the DZ and the RAF Navigator must have misjudged the exit point. Because of the error and the fact it was very windy, one soldier was blown so far off course that he landed in his next door neighbour's garden. The lady of the house was hanging her washing out at the time. She wasn't at all surprised by the sudden dropping in of her neighbour and was reputed to have said "Oh Hello, fancy seeing you here – I'll just nip in and put the kettle on!"

—CB

20
TRUE LOVE (WITH AN EXPLOSIVE ENDING)

Aldershot in the 1960s was the place to be as far as I was concerned. We were paratroopers, worked hard, drank harder and there were plenty of women. I was young and fell in love with every girl I went out with although I have to admit that I became a little disillusioned at one point and began to specialise in only married women. They cost less and knew the score. However, before I became a cynical older man, I went out with a girl called Shirley for several months. She was black haired, tall and quite beautiful – a civilian but her brother was in the Army. It was an intense romance but came to a shuddering halt when out of the blue she asked me if I was going to marry her. She then explained that if I did not want to, she was going to marry another bloke. Who? I did not know. I pointed out that I was going back to Liverpool that weekend to watch Liverpool play Aldershot in the FA Cup. A strange quirk of fate really that I was based in Aldershot yet had to travel to my home town for the match! She said she wanted an answer by the weekend and as I loved her I said I would tell her before I went. Of course, I forgot and went to Liverpool that weekend for the match. An awful performance although we won luckily. When I got back on the Monday I went around to see Shirley. Her Mum opened the door and informed me that Shirley had married on Saturday and gone to Germany with her new husband! I was astounded, hurt, felt rejected and could not believe it. I went through all the emotions and then began to plan. The following weekend was

Easter weekend and we had leave for the three days and so on Good Friday I dressed smartly in boots, puttees, denison(Para) smock and red beret and headed for Germany. I gave the keys of my room to a friend, another Cpl Thompson, an Irishman who asked if he could use it whilst I was away. Shirley's mother had explained that Shirley's new husband was an ACC Sgt attached to a regiment in Dortmund and she had given me his name. I had one small problem – I had misplaced my Military ID card but had a Passport so it did not seem a problem to me at that time.

I hitch-hiked to Dover, caught the ferry, and hitchhiked through France and Belgium and then Germany. Lifts came easily and 22 hours later I was standing outside his regiment's guardroom in Dortmund. I had forgotten that it was Easter and, of course, the regiment was on leave with only a small token guard in the guardroom. Fortunately, the Guard Commander, to whom I explained I was an old friend of the Sgts, knew who he was and where he was living as he had been on duty when they had come from the UK. He had one of his men drop me off outside the "panzer type barrack block married quarters" and I made my way up 48 stairs (I remember counting them as I practised in my mind what I was going to say to Shirley). Nothing ventured, nothing gained! Outside her door I paused then hammered on the door. A minute went by and then the door opened. I just knew it would be her that would open the door and, of course, it was. She was beautiful and at that moment I loved her immensely. She stood there, stared at me and I stared at her. She said "Oh, hello" and all my fine words evaporated. I dug my hand in my denison smock pocket, pulled out a pair of black leather gloves she had left in my car at some stage and handed them to her saying "you left these". She took them, said "thank you" and shut the door. I turned around and with my heart breaking went downstairs and headed back to the

United Kingdom! I went back via the same guardroom and helpful guard commander who arranged for me to get some tax-free cigarettes from their NAAFI and then still feeling heart-broken began hitch-hiking again. Germany was not a problem but then it all seemed to go wrong. In Belgium, just outside Mons, I was dropped off by one driver outside a military barracks and approached their guardroom thinking I may be welcomed and get a meal or whatever. I was young and did not really consider how they would feel on seeing an obvious foreign soldier wearing combat kit walking into their camp. My unit flashes on the smock were, by coincidence, the same as the Belgium flag! I was arrested, put in one of their cells. stripped of my clothing other than underpants and string vest and interrogated in broken English. They wanted to see my Military ID Card and were very unhappy that I did not have one!

Unbelievably at about four in the morning a soldier came to the cell window and whispered to me that if I wanted to go they would let me escape. I was dressed in string vest and underpants. I looked at the weapon he was holding, I looked at the field I would be crossing in moonlight and then totally ignored him. I still think it was my only wise move of the entire trip. At about eight the next morning an officer appeared who, in immaculate English, explained that they were still very unhappy with me regarding my not having an ID card but would let me go. I had all my clothes returned, dressed and they walked me to the front gates. I had been given back my tax-free cigarettes but the small amount of money I was carrying had vanished. I arrived at Calais late that night, missing the ferry and ending up sleeping in a quayside telephone box. Not recommended, I assure you. I then spent the following day trying to trade my cigarettes for a ferry ticket to Dover. Eventually I managed to barter with a local docker, got the ferry that night and landed in Dover, money-less, cigarette-less and woman-less. I have had better trips abroad. By the time I got back to Aldershot I was a day late back from leave but was extremely surprised to be arrested as I walked into Arnhem Barracks. Two men from the Military SIB approached me and led me off to a small room where everything was explained to me. I think it probably is better explained as a living nightmare. My being a day late was of no consequence to them – it did not register on their scale of misdemeanours at all. To sum up, whilst I was away, my namesake with the key to my door, Cpl Paddy Thompson, had used my bunk on the Friday evening, then travelled home to Belfast on the Saturday morning. Early hours Sunday morning he had been arrested, intoxicated, running around a telephone box he had blown up! Apparently using plastic explosive wrapped around its base. The Belfast police had found my key on him and contacted the SIB. Then I realised where this interrogation was heading. Under my bed I had a box of "odds and sods" (namely, spare ammo, pyrotechnics like thunder flashes, etc). Naturally this was against the rules but most Cpls held a little to use as extras on certain exercises. Everyone did it, knew about it but never spoke about it. It was the first thing the SIB had found! I saw my career go. An automatic Court Martial, reduced to the ranks and probably thrown out. That was my future. I was then charged by the SIB with several offences and as an afterthought they also tacked on my being AWOL for the day (Absent Without Leave). At the time my 2IC was a man called Dobson-Youngman, Captain Dobson-Youngman, known to all as DY. (There is another article in this book, written by an old friend of mine who has a different point of view of the man). However, I will be eternally grateful to DY and I will always consider him far more astute than he was given credit for. A few days later I was marched in front of DY and the charges were read out by the Sergeant Major. DY then spoke before I had time to say anything, raising his hand and telling me to be quiet. He explained that it was an automatic court martial if the ammo and pyrotechnics, found in my room, were mine. I was painfully aware of this. He then pointed out that Cpl Paddy Thompson was in Belfast prison and that, he DY, had been told by the Belfast authorities that Thompson was guaranteed at least 18 months prison for the telephone box explosion. He said that although Paddy was a good friend of mine there was therefore no point in my defending him any further! I would achieve nothing by stressing the ammo, etc, was not his! Up to that point, I had had no idea about what to do or say. I knew they were mine, DY knew they were mine; the Sergeant Major knew they were mine. The whole camp knew they were mine. I mumbled something, probably along the lines of "thirty pieces of silver" and then DY dismissed all the charges. However, he did me for being Absent Without Leave for the day. He threw a wobbler and left me in no doubt what would happen if I ever was AWOL again, etc, etc. I left that room at the double but floating on air! This is the sort of heartache my romances always seemed to bring about! Of course, this time I mentally blamed Shirley!

—JT

21
A VERY LUCKY PARACHUTIST

I'm really very lucky to be alive! Parachuting as a Paratrooper with the 16th Parachute Brigade in the 1960s and 70s was, literally, almost the death of me! I suppose I just wasn't a very good parachutist. Certainly the RAF Sergeant Instructor who taught me on the Regular Army Basic Parachute Course at The Parachute Training School at Royal Air Force Abingdon during February and March 1964, thought so. He despaired of me, or so he said at least once each day during the six weeks of the course. "My exits were terrible, my landings were worse" Fortunately at this stage we were not yet jumping from planes but only from various pieces of equipment in a very large hangar. Somehow I avoided injury while others were not so lucky, as minor injuries, mainly ankle sprains, took their toll of our numbers. Then the day came when we had to do our first jumps. These were to be from a cage hanging below a static balloon floating over the DZ (Dropping Zone) at RAF Weston-on-the-Green. We formed up in groups of five to take our turn. I was in the last stick and due to jump at No 4. In the previous balloon there had been a refusal – a Gunner in the 7th Parachute Regiment Royal Horse Artillery – had frozen in the door. He had been quickly dragged back into his corner of the balloon cage, whilst the instructors despatched the other paratroopers. When the balloon landed he was very swiftly bundled out and by the time we returned to RAF Abingdon he had gone. We now entered the balloon with our RAF PJI

(Parachute Jumping Instructor) and were quickly winched to eight hundred feet. Numbers one to three exited smoothly and then it was my turn. I was told to move forward into the door. As I had been taught I grasped the sides ready to jump into eight hundred feet of Oxford countryside when, first the PJI removed the bar across the door which was, in fact, simply a gap in the side of the balloon and secondly when he tapped my shoulder and shouted "Go" very, very loudly in my ear. Over the past six weeks we had been conditioned to jump without thinking once we heard the command "Go". The bar was duly removed. I stood in the door. I tried very hard not to look down but to look out. Quickly the command "Go" was made. I duly jumped. Almost immediately I heard my instructor shout, "That was a f— awful exit, Robinson, come back at once and do it again". Would that I could but at this point my feet had appeared in front of my eyes just at the same moment that my parachute opened. My feet then duly disappeared to take their normal position as I hung below my blessed open parachute and made, so I was told later, a quite reasonable landing. Over the next weeks I completed the further seven jumps, one more from the balloon, six from an aircraft, a Hastings, the last jump being at night, to qualify as a Paratrooper. I then joined the 16th Parachute Brigade in Nicosia, Cyprus. Elements of 16th Parachute Brigade formed around The 1st Battalion Parachute Regiment (1 PARA) had flown out on New Year's day 1964 in an attempt to stop the Greeks and the Turks killing each other. Because I was still in training at that time I did not join the Brigade until after the completion of the Parachute Course. Shortly after my arrival in Nicosia I was to do a continuation jump. All paratroopers constantly hone their parachuting skills to be ready for any operational task that may occur, with continuation training. This jump was also to be from a Hastings aircraft of the RAF. A Hasting could take two sticks of fifteen fully equipped paratroopers, however on this occasion we were only jumping in single sticks of three men. I was the third man. The third man not only held the strop of the man in front but he also held his own. Thus as I waited for the commands, "Red On, Green On, Go" I held the two strops in one hand, the other grasped my equipment I.e. the parachute weapons container strapped to my leg which contained all I needed once I hit the ground. The command duly came, the first man disappeared out of the door, then the second, then it was my turn. I threw the strops away from me, turned right into the door and jumped. Immediately I knew that something was wrong. As a rode the slip stream I felt something sliding between my arm and my body. Then there was a heavy blow on my shoulder and I was spun around before my parachute had opened. Fortunately it did open and I drifted safely to the ground. As I was to learn later I had been extremely lucky. What had happened was that although I had thrown the strops away as my left came back the strop of the man in front had caught under my arm. Thus as I exited the aircraft I was actually sliding down the strop and could, quite easily, have become entangled with the bags that flap in the slipstream of the plane, until pulled in by the PJI after all the stick have jumped. Had I been the last man in a full stick of 15 it would probably have been very, very different. My next mishap was some years later. 1974 to be exact and by co-incidence also in Cyprus. In 1964 I had been a young Lance-Corporal. In 1974 I was now a Warrant Officer First Class (WO1). We were on exercise in Cyprus, based in Dhekelia and as part of the exercise we were due to jump on the salt pans at Akrotiri, emplaning from RAF Akrotiri. We were scheduled to jump very early in the morning, about 0500 hours before the prevailing winds made parachuting too dangerous. On this jump we were to parachute from a Hercules aircraft. The Hercules was now the workhorse of the RAF. It could carry 64 fully laden paratroopers, twice as many as the Hastings, one of several aircraft it had replaced. The aircraft was carrying the full load of 64 paratroopers one of which was a Priest, a Roman Catholic Padre who was 16 Parachute Brigade's Padre. He was opposite me in the aircraft which made me feel quite warm and safe. Who better to have opposite you than one of the Good Lord's servants. Unfortunately it didn't quite work out like that.

I exited the aircraft to a sky full of other paratroopers. I carried out the normal drills, I.e. I looked up to make sure that my parachute had opened correctly. It had! I looked around to make sure that I wasn't in danger of entangling with any other jumper. I wasn't! I then lowered my weapons container, grasped the strops and prepared for my landing. Then, bang, a pair of boots smashed into my face followed by the legs they supported and I found myself looking into the face of the Padre. We had very little time before we hit the ground. We both tried to free ourselves but couldn't. His parachute was partially collapsed and thus we were travelling a lot faster than was safe. Another, bang. This time it was the ground. In seconds other paratroopers rushed over to us. We actually landed about fifteen metres apart. We were both semi-conscious but miraculously not seriously injured. My nose didn't look too pretty. Later I was diagnosed with a hairline fracture of the upper jaw and a bent coccyx – which nearly forty years later, still gives me problems. The Padre suffered similar injuries. We were very, very lucky indeed. My parachuting days ended in 1975 when I left 16 Parachute Brigade on commissioning. I have not been tempted to parachute since!

—CR

IN THE 1970s

22
SOUTH KOREA

In the mid-1970s I served in South Korea wearing two hats. I worked in the British Embassy with a Brigadier in the Defence Attaches Office which dealt with all military matters with the South Korean and American Military. Both of us were also members of the four man British permanent element of the Commonwealth Liaison Mission (CLM) (The two other personnel were a RAPC Pay Sgt and a REME Mechanic). The four of us, plus an Honour Guard of approximately sixty British troops from Hong Kong, helped by the 42,000 American troops also based in Seoul and the South Korean Army had, as our first job, to stop the North Korean forces if or when they invaded and then wait for reinforcements!

In our job as representing the CLM, the Brigadier and I attended the Military Armistice Commission meetings in Panmunjom, the demilitarized zone (DMZ), monthly or whenever an incident occurred. This entailed four North Korean Generals and a Chinese General sitting on one side of a large oak table which straddled the 38th Parallel Line. On our side of the table two South Korean Generals, two American Generals and my Brigadier (As a 1 star General) sat facing them. In theory, whatever was on the agenda was then discussed. I sat behind the Brigadier which allowed me a lot of scope for relaxing. You needed to relax as every meeting began with a mandatory two to three hours of martial music and a tirade of abuse in Korean and English (American edition) blasted at you from the speakers on their side of the room and on their side of the compound in which our building was centrally located. On a bad day, they would harangue us for five, six, seven or eight hours! Each time, the main reason for the meeting having been called, may or may not have been mentioned at some point in the day but I often left a 12 hour meeting not knowing what the reason had been for the meeting and what the hell had been discussed. I am sure, everyone else did likewise.

A major concern for both sides was that they could not be seen to be out manoeuvred in any way and this was often reflected in these meetings. If, as at one meeting, it had been decided that there were to be a set number of ashtrays, pens, blotting pads, place mats, etc on each side of the table and a set number of flags at each end of the room, inevitably one side attempted to bring bigger ashtrays and extra drinking glasses to the next meeting, There was protests of course but then the wronged side brought bigger ashtrays, etc, to the next meeting and so on. Whilst I was there and over several meetings the North Korean Flag mysteriously grew to perhaps five times its normal size, then the South Korean began to do the same but with a little extra height each time! Eventually another meeting was called just to resolve this! You didn't need nuclear weapons or disarmament on the agenda when you had important subjects like this to discuss!

My over-riding impression of these meetings however was how impressive the American Honour Guard was as it was mandatory that all of the men in it were at least 6′ 2″ at least seventeen stone, wore immaculate uniform and all wore white helmets with MP emblazoned on them. They paraded along our side of the 38th Parallel Line in the village whilst the 4′ 11″ inch North Korean Honour Guard in their 1950s Chinese Communist style too-large uniforms paraded the other side. It was no contest in appearances! However, looks can be deceiving as several months later several members of the North Korean Honour Guard whilst on parade attacked the American 2IC and his Second Lieutenant and brutally axed them to death. It led right up to the brink of full-scale war with America moving aircraft carriers and squadrons very quickly towards Korea. Happily it did not start another war as even Kim Il Sung, the North Korean leader, although clearly mad, realised they had gone too far and he issued an apology and regret over the incident.

Strangely enough, the only fighting I saw in Korea was between the American Honour Guard, the South Korean Honour Guard and the British Honour Guard who happened to be the Kings Regiment, Liverpool, at that time. We were summoned, the Brigadier and I, by the American Military Police and arrived at the communal barracks where sixty of the Kings were defending a couple of accommodation blocks against the South Korean and American combined forces. It was about two in the morning. Windows were already broken, the odd door had been smashed, fire buckets and their contents were everywhere and it appeared to be becoming very serious. I was armed with the inevitable pick-axe handle and the Brigadier in his uniform. The uniform saved the day! Neither the Americans nor the South Koreans felt they could attack a General and went back to their barracks and with no one to fight the Kings Regiment went back to their serious drinking! I never did find out what had happened but everyone's honour seemed satisfied so it was never mentioned again. After all, Korea is known as "the Land of the Morning Calm"! Although this was the only physical fighting I was involved in there, there was, of course, the inevitable on-going power struggle within the Embassy. The FCOs dislike of all things military and our loathing of what they appeared to represent did not make for good bedfellows. We had our office in the secure section of their

Chancery and admittance into the area was through a controlled barred door. Quite a secure area. One morning I came into work and before I had even entered our office I was accosted by the First Secretary who with an obscene smirk on his face informed me that he had bad news for me. He was a man, hated by everyone in the Embassy, whose sole aim in life was to move up the ladder as quickly as possible using everyone else as a rung. He had been passing our office earlier, minutes after the Brigadier had left it to go to a meeting at the American Embassy, and he "could not help but notice," (his words) that a Top Secret document was lying in the Brigadier's Out Tray. It was in a totally secure area as I have said but it was a cardinal sin as far as the First Secretary was concerned. Anyway he pointed out he would decide what to do by the following morning although he was certain he would have to report it to the UK.

I did not see the Brigadier for the rest of that day and the next morning I went in early with the intention of seeing the First Secretary and appealing to the good side of his nature; although I knew there wasn't one! I went to his office, which was empty, and there on his desk was a 'Top Secret' stamped file! It took possibly thirty seconds for that file to move to our office safe! It was not the original file but it was a much shaken First Secretary who, half an hour later appeared at our office. We traded Top Secret files, as you do, and naturally I said I would not be reporting it as he assured me that he had never had that intention anyway. He left rather unhappily and I spent the rest of my tour there watching him like a hawk. The Brigadier never knew about this incident as like everything Top Secret it was on a "need to know" basis!

In the year the Brigadier and I spent in the Embassy we did achieve one very notable success after putting heart and soul into trying to sell the South Korean Military British weapons.

We had our own contacts in their Military and also a few shady characters who seemed to know everyone and who we often wined and dined. In fact, for a little while we thought we were well on the way to selling them our Rapier Ground-to-Air missile system. We had ensured we were experts on its capabilities as the sale would have meant millions of pounds for Britain. However, it eventually dawned on us that the ROK Military were basically funded by the USA and they were selling/leasing them Redeye, their equivalent to Rapier. We had had no chance! Fortunately, we managed to save our reputation as international arms dealers by locating an old 25 pounder artillery gun in a Hong Kong scrapyard, getting it reconditioned and sent to us in Korea! The South Koreans wanted one for their Military Museum – I think they offered the equivalent of £500. We suggested we give it as a gift: naturally the MOD accepted the money! Thirty odd years later, looking back you could say we weren't very good arms salesmen but at least that four man team in the Commonwealth Liaison Mission must have done some good and perhaps still is doing some good – there hasn't been a war there since. Mind you, I am not sure if they ever let the Kings Regiment back there as the Honour Guard.

—JT

23
FORGIVE BUT DO NOT FORGET

In the mid 1960s we, as a parachute brigade moved into a custom built camp in the middle of Aldershot. It was an open camp, as most were in those days, which meant literally anyone could wander through the barracks. This all changed quite dramatically with an unexpected and obscene bombing by the Official IRA on the 22nd February 1972. One or more of these brave individuals in the name of the RC population of Northern Ireland parked a car full of explosive outside the HQ Parachute Brigade Officers Mess.

They managed to explode it, quite incompetently, whilst the building was unoccupied by any military personnel but contained only civilian staff. Seven civilians were killed, which included five women kitchen workers and one elderly gardener. The other "kill" they could claim was Father Gerard Weston – an Irish Roman Catholic!

I was possibly the third person to reach the devastated area on that day and on my subsequent four month tours in Northern Ireland that obscenity was always in my mind. Looking back, I can only marvel at how restrained we were. I have, over the years, from time to time, wondered how the murderers lived with themselves. It could not have been easy!

—JT

24

PARACHUTING – THE MAYOR OF GRAYS, ESSEX

It was a lovely sunny afternoon in the early 1970s when Gerald gunned the twin engines of the ancient De Havilland Rapide and accelerated along the grass runway of Netheravon Airfield in Wiltshire. On board was a merry band of free-fall parachute 'nuts' embarking on a long transit to the East End of London – Grays, Essex to be precise – to perform another death-defying feat as part of the annual Grays Carnival.

Though we were blessed with big blue skies, the wind was increasing and as we reached west London and started to cross the metropolis, conditions became very bumpy. One of our number that day was Trish, a lively and engaging young captain in Queen Alexandra's Royal Army Nursing Corps. Trish, in those days, was one of the few women in the country qualified to take part in free-fall displays and she was well versed in the business. Experience however, did not exempt her from air-sickness and on that day, she spent much of our final run-in to the dropping zone, with her head sticking out of the open 'jump' door being violently ill.

With two minutes to go, Trish was looking very pale and wan but insisted that she was ok to jump. With some tissues from Gerald our intrepid aviator, we cleaned Trish's lovely visage and made her presentable. A quick final equipment check and our band of eight exited the aircraft and two or three minutes later we were landing in the centre of the arena to rapturous applause from the large crowd. As standard practice, military free-fall teams always do a line-up at the end of a display and are then introduced to the senior VIP present. That day, we were presented to the Mayor of Grays.

Mayors come in all shapes, sizes with varying degrees of style. The Mayor that day was a little like Arthur Daley meets James Bond. He greeted us with great, hand-pumping enthusiasm until he spotted, as the last person in the line-up – Trish. By now Trish had recovered some of her colour and was exuding her normal beauty. Without hesitating, Mr Mayor pounced, gripped Trish around her slim waist and in a flash had her in what could be called a "lip-lock" and what he was doing with his tongue we'll never know. Nobody had the heart to tell him that only six minutes beforehand, the lovely Trish had been regurgitating for England. There is no moral to this tale but it still makes me chuckle.

—PO'C

25

PARACHUTING – BSM YORKIE CHALLINOR 7 PARA REGT RHA

Yorkie was an accomplished free-fall parachutist and was a member of a 16-man team from the Rhine Army Parachute Association chosen to provide a display as part of the 1977 Queen's Jubilee Review of the British Army of the Rhine.

A part of the plan was that, immediately following the jump, the team should line up to meet the Queen. During the dress rehearsal on 6th July 1977, we were briefed by a member of the Royal Household on protocol. We were told to address the Queen as "Your Majesty" on first meeting and thereafter as "Ma'am" (as in jam).

The great day arrived and 16 intrepid skydivers jumped from 4,500 feet (the cloudbase precluded the planned 12,000 foot exit), landed in the arena and quickly made their way to the line-up point where they were to meet HM.

I was standing next to Yorkie as the Queen approached us. She said, "Have you chaps just parachuted?" and Yorkie bowed his head and said "Yes, sir"

—PO'C

26
SURVEILLANCE – THE GOLDEN RULES

For short periods being involved in the tracing or watching of people can be a deeply rewarding experience and you discover many things about the human race. However, it does take expertise and normally a great deal of teamwork. Sometimes you see or hear things that are beyond comprehension. There are, of course, some golden rules when carrying out surveillance. The most important being that you ALWAYS attempt to remain "the grey man". You blend in with the local scene, do nothing that is out of the ordinary and wear nothing out of the ordinary. Also, never be surprised by anything.

Two things brought this home to me vividly. One was in Northern Island when we first operated there in the 1970s. We had watched a man for four days believing he was a terrorist. We had followed him and at night we had a perfect view of his farmhouse. In the early hours of the fifth morning he came out of his farmhouse, carrying a shovel and went into the middle of a nearby field and began digging.

He spent 10 to 15 minutes creating a hole and then pulled out of the ground a large object. Naturally we thought: "Weapons"! We knew only one way to deal with terrorists holding weapons!

He unwrapped the parcel and produced a fiddle! Whilst we were hidden there he either consciously or unconsciously serenaded us with what I can only describe as an ear-wrenching din. I have hated the instrument ever since.

Looking back over the years, I have often wondered if the man ever knew how close he had come to playing his own "lament"!

The second incident happened in the early 1980s when, having left the Army, I was working for a security firm in London. These firms were of varying quality: some employed trained, experienced people and some did not. They sent me to join a team carrying out surveillance on a couple living in the North. As we were going out for the first covert checking of the hotel which the couple ran, my compatriot turned up in yellow socks, yellow gloves and four inch heels on his cut away cowboy boots. It sounded like I was leading a horse around the dark quiet roads of Morecambe. He was not ex-Special Forces! I only stayed there that night and then resigned from the job!

—JT

27

PARACHUTING – OPERATION DROP OUT

This should have been my first night parachute drop. But jumping into North Unst, Shetlands, it was still light at two in the morning. I was first out of the Hercules door and still over the sea, but the wind drifted me onto the narrow peninsular. After a good landing I was unwrapping my Bergen (rucksack) as the next drop came in when I heard a dull thud within yards of me and saw a machete sticking in the ground. Some clot had jumped with it tucked down the side of his Bergen and it had fallen out: definitely a close thing. I watched the others exiting from the aircraft with a bit more interest; just as well, as a Bergen detached itself from a jumper and fell to earth, again missing those on the ground.

But its contents weren't so lucky. His rifle was bent like a banana, and the radio had reverted to its component parts and rattled like a model T Ford. Parachuting is relatively safe. Drop Zones are not! I left the DZ rather quickly, thinking "what an appropriate name for a parachuting exercise!"

—AS

28
LET ME ENTERTAIN YOU

Two well known staff clerks from HQ 16 Para Bde were posted to Bahrain in 1969/70. Bahrain was due to close down in December 1971 and these two scallywags spent their last few weeks in Bahrain living in the RAF Muharraq Sgts Mess.

For those not acquainted with the RAF, the members of RAF Sgts Messes tend to be very old compared to army messes and our two scallywags were new to the mess and in their early twenties.

By October 1971 all the families had been repatriated to the UK and only the servicemen remained. Therefore there were no wives or other women living in or around the service environment. Our two friends, EC and DG were living in the RAF Mess.

The only form of evening entertainment was the cinema and then the bar. Evenings were therefore duly spent in this way. One evening EC and DG returned to the bar from the cinema. The RAF Argosy Squadron were due to leave Bahrain the following day and a huge party was in progress. At this point we have to explain that the Argosy Squadron were visitors and were despised almost as much as the army chaps living in the RAF Mess.

EC and DG duly decided the best place to spend the evening was with the Argosy crews. After far too much beer the departing Argosy Squadron lads decided to entertain the whole mess, which must have had around 100 men and only one woman present, who was a stewardess from the daily VC10 flight returning soldiers/airmen to the UK.

The Argosy Squadron lads duly got onto the dance floor and did their drunken version of Old MacDonald's farm. This went down a treat. However, our young Sgt DG had a reputation for performing Zulu Warrior and one glance at Sgt EC proved telepathy does work! As soon as the RAF lads had finished Old Macdonald, Sgts EC and DG went onto the dance floor and began Zulu Warrior.

The Station Warrant Office immediately approached the one lady in the mess and asked her to leave. Her reply was a definite NO! EC and DG began Zulu Warrior and went down a treat.

The following morning, Saturday, after work EC and DG went to the mess for a life saving lunch time pint of shandy. Standing at the centre of the bar was the Station Warrant Officer and his cohorts. Remember the age of the RAF Mess members. This very senior, and old, WO walked to the centre of the room, and summoned our two young Sgts to his presence.

As they approached, the two young lads thought, "Oh no, this is it, we will be banished from the mess to the army Sgts Mess".

"Right you two" said the Stn WO in his loudest sergeant major voice. "I want a word with you about last night!" Oh dear, here it comes they thought.

The Stn WO continued, "About last night, (long pause, stern look) that's the best entertainment we've had in here for ages!"

—DG

29
TO CRACK A NUT

One night up in London, Lt Col Keith… The Commanding Officer was briefing his boys on a forthcoming task. A Scandinavian Government had asked the FCO to help them out with their annual security exercise. They were going to call up their Reservist Forces and task them to secure the national ammunition compound, and the ammunition, against possible sabotage by the British Special Forces. The Regiment had no problem with their plan to free-fall in at night, the electric fences and guard dogs could also be dealt with… And they could actually gain entry fairly simply, and likewise exit. The problem was that all the ammunition bunkers were deep underground, and the only entry/exit was via a huge circular steel door, which was operated by tumbler locks and a secure code. Lt Col Keith… Was pushing this problem round the table but nobody could work out how to crack an unknown code? Just then young "Billy" turned up very late… "Sorry Boss, working late on the Building Site… So what's the problem?" He was briefed… "OK, got it…. Simple really." They took his advice, parachuted in, did what they had to do, got out, and came back to UK. The Scandinavian Government went ape-sh*t! When they had gained entry to the compound, Billy went to the big security door, and poured quick drying cement into the locks. Now nobody could get in… But worse still… The Scandinavians could not get in either to get their ammo... So simple and innocent really...

—AM

30

RHEINDAHLEN HOLIDAY CAMP - DRINKING AND NOT DRIVING

I remember my days in Rheindahlen in the 1970s with fond memories. I tend to think of it as a bit of a holiday camp, not too much work, plenty of amenities, big NAAFI and lots of sport. Saturdays were spent playing rugby for the Rhinos. The drill was that Carol and the kids would come and watch the last ten minutes. After the game it was straight to the club house for a few beers. The kids would get a free meal here. After a couple of pints we went off home, organised the baby sitter and were in the Sgts Mess for 20:30 where a busy social night would ensue.

The Sgts Mess was approximately one mile from our quarter, and in between was the RAF Sgts Mess and no less than SIX officers' messes. Remember that in Germany you don't even consider having a drink and then driving !

Around 01:00 we would wander off home and stop off at the RAF Mess. Another couple of drinks were dispatched here. Then it was time to stroll/stagger the last half mile home, past all the officers' messes.

One Monday morning, when I was CC G Ops, my boss breezed into the office whilst I was opening up. "Good Morning Chief", "Good Morning Sir".

"You had a good night on Saturday, Chief?" "Yes, sir." I replied, thinking how the hell does he know that? "I thought so, I nearly ran you over twice."

—DG

31

SOLDIERS AND CREDIT

Scene, army camp in Germany, 1970. Soldiers get very easy credit from the NAAFI and Local German Banks. In most units soldiers need the Admin Officer's written authority to purchase, on credit, a large item like a car.

One day a well known young miscreant in my unit was seen driving around barracks in a brand new car. Let's call the miscreant Pte B. I called him into my office, with the Pay Sgt present and having checked how much Pte B was paid each month (DM 1000). I had also read Private B's file beforehand and checked his authorisation note.

I then said to Pte B, "I see you're driving a brand new car, presumably you paid cash for it?" Pte B "No, sir." DG "No, then how did you pay for it?" Pte B "I got it on credit." DG "And who signed the authorisation." Pte B "You did, sir." DG "Sorry, no chance, not with you."

Pte B "Yes sir, you did." DG "Definitely not." Pte B "I know you too well." I then opened his file and showed him the authorisation certificate. "Pte B whose signature is that". Pte B "Sgt A, he signed it whilst the unit were on exercise." DG "Ah ! Now we are getting somewhere. Right, how much is the monthly payment?" Pte B "DM500, sir." DG "DM500! That's half your pay ! OK, and what happened to the old banger you had when you arrived here?" Pte B "Oh, I've still got that, sir" DG "Presumably there is no outstanding finance on that car" Pte B "Oh yes, sir, just DM300 per month." DG "Just DM300 per month!" Pte B "Yes, sir." DG "So you bought that to come to Germany?" Pte B "Yes, sir." DG "And did you have a previous car before that?" Pte B "Yes, sir." DG " Any finance owing on that?" Pte B "Yes, sir". DG "Oh my god! How much?" Pte B "DM200, sir." DG "Three cars, DM1000 payments, Pte B, can you see we have a problem here?" Pte B "No, sir."

OMG! End of interview. DG takes a long walk outside! Then proceeds to find a job for Pte B's wife so they can afford to shop for food.

—DG

32

THE MINEFIELD GAP BAOR

Having slogged for hours building a barrier minefield parallel to, and seemingly as long as, the River Leine, the RE Field Troop from Osnabruck settled down to police the minefield gaps which, on orders, had been closed by notional cratering. But because this was a German public road the only visible sign of an obstruction was a white mine tape cross on the road. Shortly after dawn, a troop of four Chieftain tanks bearing orange forces markings thundered up, and were only prevented from charging through the obstruction by a very determined Troop Staff Sergeant (SSgt) planting himself on the cross and raising both hands to halt the 70 ton monsters. The lead tank commander, an aristocratic young man from a fractional Hussar regiment, leaned out from his turret and politely asked what the hold-up was... On being told about the obstruction, he opined that the white tape cross did not even vaguely look like a crater. The SSgt, fairly forcefully asked him to imagine there was indeed a big hole in the road which he couldn't cross. The 'fash' cav officer responded "Staff... If you want me to imagine that's a hole" said he, pointing languidly at the white tape, and then slapping his tank "I want you to imagine this is a helicopter!" With a big grin and a 'fly on pilot' to his driver he shot through the gap followed by the rest of his grinning troop!

—CW

33
THE GUARDSMAN'S BURDEN

As a Royal Engineer Search Adviser in Northern Ireland I was supervising a large search operation involving both RE and Infantry search teams in a very dodgy area of Belfast. The cordon surrounding the area was provided by a Guards Battalion. Whilst standing alongside the cordon commander, a fresh faced Guards Subaltern, I noticed that his holstered pistol butt had a very garish, almost luminous green bit protruding. Curious, I asked him about it. He fished out the weapon, a green plastic water pistol, produced a little squirt and told me that since he had nearly had a negligent discharge recently his Platoon Sergeant had banned him from carrying any firearm again. The said Platoon Sergeant shrugged his shoulders…grinned and said "He'll be very good… Someday… But right now he's a guardsman's burden!" He probably became a General…

—CW

34
WEETABIX

A famous RE RSM was known as 'Mick the nick' for his habit of jailing anybody who even looked like he was contemplating kicking over the traces and was not known as a particularly insightful man.

When one of our young female drivers from the WRAC detachment badly upset him she wound up in the Guardroom overnight and when the guard commander reported to the RSM the following morning, he was asked how the girl had fared. The guard commander told him that she had sobered up nicely and that her only request had been for Tampax. The RSM barked at him "Tell her she can have bloody Weetabix like everybody else!"

—CW

35
A CRY IN THE DARK

We had suffered weeks of living in tents and trenches in the middle of Salisbury Plain in midwinter. As the HQ of a Para Bn Group we had jumped onto Everleigh DZ and moved forward to positions previously recced by our Pathfinder Company. In theory, we were in Germany and were in position to engage the red hordes when they attacked. In practice, we were in a freezing, dismal, water-logged and barren area near Andover. Every bit of our kit was soaked through and endurance and perseverance had been tested to the limit.

At last we were pulled out and our group huddled in our wet kit into our even wetter sleeping bags in the back of a three tonner and started to drift into our own little worlds as the truck set off for the long journey to Aldershot.

However everyone's attention was quickly attracted by an officer sitting next to me who began to loudly reminisce about his experience of being invited the previous month to dinner with the Queen. He had been Officer of the Guard at Buckingham Palace for several months as his Battalion had been on duty there. On his final evening he attended the Palace where he was ushered into the dining room with six other guests. He was in his best Service Dress, medals, etc and the Queen sat at the head of the table with the Duke of Edinburgh at the other end. There was a huge log fire, the room was beautiful and warm and his description of the dinner, the drinks, the sweet and the entire evening was as detailed as it was entrancing. Suddenly, however, as he began to describe the cigars and after meal drinks, he was cut short as from the back of the pitch dark three tonner an agonized voice called:

"For God's sake, boss, that's all very well but they weren't happy, were they? Not like we are now!"

—JT

36
A FALLEN HERO

When serving in the Commonwealth Liaison Mission in South Korea in the '70s, I discovered the American Army of 42,000 troops based there had an eight-man Special Forces Detachment living quite near our Compound in Seoul. They were the oddest group of soldiers I have ever met. Their OC was a French Canadian who, in my more generous moments, I merely considered insane. All eight had moved directly to Korea from Vietnam after the war there finished. None had gone back to the United States or to their families there and all had a Korean "wife" living with them in their Compound. After a few beers each would explain that although they loved their USA wife, they found it easier to leave her in America and live with their Korean counterpart. I never could understand the language the OC spoke although I quickly noticed that he left the bar each night at about 7pm, complete with rifle. I found out sometime later that because South Korea was still technically at war with the North, there was a nightly curfew and he liked to go out, on his own, and deal with any offenders. I did not want to know any more details or to meet him on a dark night! All of them were grossly overweight, by British standards and the metal bar stools in their little Mess were replaced virtually monthly as misshapen wrecks. They all felt enormously let down by the US Government. Years later, when "MASH" was a great hit on TV, I could not help but compare some of the characters. They seemed so very similar. I liked them though. They never seemed to argue with each other, were good company to drink with, extremely generous to us impoverished Brits and also liked the Brits. What else do you want? They all felt they had done their basic training and continuation training in Vietnam under fairly arduous conditions and therefore they did not need anymore! However, the one thing they did seem to enjoy next to drinking was parachuting which they appeared to do regularly and so this is where my story begins... The Brigadier and I were both ex-Parachute Brigade so I went to see their Detachment, officially, to ask if we could jump with them. I had already ensured the MOD agreement by telling them that the Americans had requested we parachute with them. The OC was delighted, I think, and a week later I had a phone call and went off to their place to report in. The Brigadier was unfortunately away but I was determined to not lose the opportunity.

They had their own Huey UH-1H helicopter and packed their own 'chutes, so we were off parachuting quite quickly. It went well and I was invited to come along the following day. This time when I got there, I noticed a huge good-looking dog standing rather reluctantly next to the helicopter. It had a collar on it with inverted American Sgt stripes and one of the blokes explained that it was the detachment dog and he would be parachuting with us. His name was Hero and as I was a Briton and naturally loved animals! the dog would lie across my lap before parachuting. We fitted parachutes and Hero was fitted with his. We then boarded the heli and three of us sat on the floor edge, facing outwards with our feet on the ski-type landing bars (technical description?). The dog, not totally willingly, lay across my lap and because of its size, its front legs lay on the bloke on my left and its back legs on the bloke on my right. Not a problem. We then took off and at 1500 ft the nominated-for-the-day Jumpmaster and the most casual I have ever met, indicated that I should release the dog who, at that stage, seemed very unwilling to leave me! However, I let him go and off he went downwards and shortly after his parachute billowed out below us. We then jumped.

When I landed, the dog came bowling over to me, barking, licking me and very very happy with the World. Then to my surprise the blokes lined up and with great ceremony held a small parade and the OC presented the Sgt Hero with his "wings", pinning them on his collar above his stripes. Apparently it was Hero's 5th jump and he was therefore entitled to wear them. The parade was quite moving, in an odd way and the dog loved the attention. The following month I had another phone call from them and went off to their compound to parachute again. I was warmly welcomed and was getting my 'chutes ready when I noticed Hero over the other side of square. I called him and he seemed reluctant to come over to me and that is when I noticed that he still had his collar on but there was only one stripe on it and NO wings!

Apparently, the previous week when the heli was hovering at 1500 ft, Hero had refused to jump, clawed his way back into the heli, biting the Jumpmaster on the way and would not budge from there. When they had landed the heli the detachment had charged him with disobeying a direct order, held a drumbeat Court Martial and stripped him of his "wings" and reduced him to Cpl. It saddened me greatly as fallen heroes always do but I have never seen a happier dog.

—JT

37
THE LEGACY OF THE BRITISH RAJ

Of the many anomalies one encounters in the Service of Her Majesty, one of the most puzzling for me was that the Naval Attache on the Defence Staff of the (then) British Embassy Pakistan in the late 1970s was stationed up in the north of the country in Islamabad rather than 1500 miles south in Karachi where the Pakistani Navy (and the nearest oggin) could be found.

However, it did mean that whenever we had a ship's visit said Naval Attache and I, in my role as Staff Assistant, got to rough it for a week in the Hotel Intercontinental in Karachi. He to sort out Senior Naval Officers and local dignitaries who were being entertained in the various wardrooms, me to concentrate on the more mundane admin tasks such as sorting out the ships mail and ensuring the agent handled the victualling of ships. I also had an important unofficial task, that of publicising on-board parties to any aircrew stopping over in Karachi – a sort of pimp extraordinaire to the PO's messes. But I digress...

On this particular deployment we had HMS Antrim, HMS Coventry, RFA Stromness and an Australian patrol boat stopping in Karachi en route to Hong Kong. My first, and probably most important, task was to collect the mailbags which had been sent from BFPO Ships to Karachi airport. Because the ships were due to dock early in the morning, I decided to collect the bags the night before so that I could have them on the dockside ready to hand over as soon as the ships tied up.

I should add at this point that this was circa 1980 when General Zia ul Haq was in power. In some ways, this made life easier because wearing a uniform seemed to open doors but it also tended to make for a fairly rigid bureaucracy. I duly arrived at Karachi airport and on the strength of my ID card gained access to the military area of the airport where I was to collect the bags. It was a typical late night airport scene with the few people who were around watching portable televisions or reading newspapers. I parked up outside the mail office, went inside and announced that I had come to collect the mailbags for the named ships. I duly showed the chap on duty my ID card but this time the magic didn't work. He asked me for "my chitty" and informed me in no uncertain terms that without a chitty I could not have the mailbags.

Was all my planning going to be for nought? Was I going to be responsible for the cardinal sin of delaying delivery of the ships' mail? I had already admitted that I didn't have a chitty so I told the chap that I had some official embassy forms and asked if it was OK if I created a chitty. He said that would be OK so I went to the Consular Land Rover, praying that there was something in the vehicle papers I could use.

Lo and behold there were three or four blank transport requisition forms. So I returned with a blank form and in his presence created a chitty. In the space for "To" I wrote" Visiting Royal Navy ships" followed by the ships names; In the space marked "From" I wrote "Karachi International Airport"; In the space marked "Detail" I asked how many bags there were, to which he replied five and I wrote "five mail bags". The chitty was completed by the entry of my rank and name under "Authorised By" and then a signature.

All this had been done in the presence of a smiling official. "Cracked it" I thought! But no, after a pregnant pause he said "A stamp. The chitty must have a stamp." Looking suitably forlorn, I told him I did not have a stamp with me. I suggested we could use his stamp and I would sign on top of it to make it official. He gave me a long jobs-worth look and shook his head in disbelief but then said "OK but just this once. Next time you must bring a stamp." Hardly believing my luck I was effusive in my thanks and said the embassy would write to express our thanks that he had been so helpful.

He then handed over the mailbags which I put into the back of the Land Rover. I then asked if I would need a gate pass to get out of the secure area with the bags. He gave me another despairing look, turned the chitty over, wrote something in Urdu on the back, stamped and signed it.

Arriving at the exit, I was duly stopped and handed over the by now multi-purpose chitty to the guard who looked at it, smiled, handed it back to me and waved me through. I left in a kind of daze with both chitty and mailbags. So we did not only bequeath the railways and the Grand Trunk Road, the cult of the chitty is alive and well, if a bit surreal in application.

—DL

IN THE 1980s

38

MY FIRST ENCOUNTER WITH SPECIAL FORCES
JIM DAVIDSON OBE

John was the first SAS man that I met. It was also because of him I got to know the Regiment quite well and made lifelong friends. Unfortunately some of their lives came to a short and sudden end. It went with the job! I got to admire these special men, not just because of their toughness and heroic deeds but because of the way they conducted themselves, the way they went about their lives. They worked hard and boy, they played hard as well…don't you worry about that!! It was 1980. I had won New Faces and the world was my oyster. I had my own TV show and was a household name. This was before the PC brigade invaded of course. Combined Service Entertainment had asked me to go to Belize. I jumped at the chance. A singer called Frank Leyton, A juggler, three girl dancers and a three piece band would accompany me. The resident infantry regiment in Belize was The Cheshire's. There was also a number of RAF chappies who looked after and flew the choppers and the 4 GR1 Harriers. We were based in Belize City although the shows would be spread out over the country wherever our troops were stationed. It was hot and humid. The shows were mainly outdoors and the parties after were epic. The show at Airport camp had to be delayed by two hours because of a power cut. By the time we had finished and traipsed back to the Sgts mess the cook had finished and flatly refused to feed us. I noticed some men sitting in the corner of the near empty mess. One called me over. These guys looked tanned and fit. They wore no uniform and all had bandit moustaches. I thought they were civilian workers from the U.K. They were in-fact a group of A Squadron SAS.

We told them of our dilemma. The chef had refused to cook as we were two hours late. One guy went to see the chef. He returned with a mischievous grin and said in broad Scouse "Steak or Pork chop?" What magical powers of persuasion did he use on the chef? I asked. "I told him to cook or I'd put the nut on him" He said with a smile. Who are these guys? I was to find out three days later. Next day saw us driving down to Punta Gorda to entertain another lot of Cheshires. After the show a Cheshire Sgt asked me and Frank Leyton if we wanted to go into the town for a drink. We grabbed a Land Rover and the Sgt persuaded someone to drop us into town five kilometres away. We arrived at what was best described as a set of wriggly tin buildings with music blaring from them. Locals were hanging around smoking and drinking. We entered a big shack that was lit with ultra violet light and was greeted by eyeballs and teeth! The smell of wacky-backie was in the air and the DJ must have been smoking most of it judging by the distortion on the sound system. Frank and I shared a look of "What are we doing here?" I asked the Sgt where the driver was? "Gone home", he said "don't worry we'll get a cab back". We drank some warm beer from plastic glasses and I was introduced to a girl called Gobbling Jenny. She was the ugliest hooker in captivity. After an hour of this torture Frank and I decided that we better head for home and set out to look for our Sgt in the crowded tin hut. He had had a couple and was feeling no pain. We eventually coaxed him out of the club. He then shouted "Taxi" and leapt on a local bloke's back piggy-back style. With this, the guy shook him off and started to lay into him. Soon there were half a dozen guys kicking him. I went forward to help and a guy pulled a knife on me and strangely, shone a torch on it. I protested and said I was not a soldier. I pointed out my long hair. The gang turned to study these two strange Brits.

The Sgt took this moment of this distraction to make his move and like a well-oiled machine... ran away! The thugs turned to see where he had gone. Frank and I then ran away as well. The problem now was, to decide where to run. We were in the jungle in the middle of nowhere with a gang of knife wielding cannibals after us. We hid behind a wrecked car and took stock. We were in a sort of clearing in the jungle with five dirt roads leading off of it. The thugs were searching for the Sgt. We had to make a decision and make it fast. I turned to Frank. He was white and shaking. Shit! this is down to me. "That one" I pointed to a road and we set of. We ran as fast as we could. We had no water, and no idea where we were or where we were going. We were just running...for our lives! It was stifling hot and our hearts were pounding. After 10 minutes of flat out running we slowed down to catch our breath and to check we weren't being followed. The road had narrowed. We were in thick jungle on a gravel path covered with Land Crabs. Horrible things that could and did attack passing Land Rovers. What we would give for a Land Rover then. The sky was a mass of stars. The jungle was alive with fireflies that looked like snipers lighting fags. We were thirsty frightened and worse...someone was following us. After our initial panic I decided what to do. Firstly we covered our white shirts in mud! Secondly we broke into a trot. Every minute I counted out loud "1 2 3 stop!" On STOP we would freeze. I cocked my head ,opened my mouth and listened...Gravel footsteps! We were indeed being followed. By now our lack of water was beginning to show. Our heads were pounding. A sure sign of de-hydration. I could not swallow. I had heard that if you suck a pebble it would moisten your mouth. I bent down to pick up a stone. It bit me. It was a land crab. We had jogged for another 10 minutes or so when I grabbed Frank and threw us both into a trackside ditch. The footsteps were right behind us. We were covered in filth and rotten things! We held our breaths. The footsteps sounded like one person. We couldn't see who it was; I surmised it must have been the Sgt returning. I shouted in a large whisper "Sarge" The footsteps got quicker and passed us by. As the threat of being followed was over we crawled out of the ditch and continued on our road to nowhere. What else could we do? I noticed that there was a blank bit in the sky. Something was blocking out the stars. It was a mountain. I knew that the base was at the bottom of the mountain. All we had to do was following this track to the mountain and then circumnavigate it and we would find the base. As luck would have it the track I had chosen took us directly to the base. I was lucky in the five to one choice at the clearing. We arrived at the camp main gate and told our story to the guard. We guzzled down some water and thanked God that we had made it. In the corner of the guard-room I noticed a Gurkha. He was sweating and wide eyed. "What's up with him?" I asked. I was told that he was in the same club as us and was walking back, as you do, when he heard voices calling him from the jungle!! We quickly told our story to the military police. As we were talking the Sgt walked in. He was pissed and had a black eye.

"F—g lot of good you two were" he said and staggered off to bed! Many years later I had suffered a horrendous drive of 11 hours through the mountains of Bosnia. It was the day after Boxing Day. It was wet and freezing. I was hung over and knackered. We stopped at the army camp in Vitez. Someone opened the door for me and in the dark I heard a voice. "I bet you don't f—g remember me" Oh yes I did! Anyway back to Belize.

We had been out to an Island called San Pedro. It was idyllic after the dirty Belize jungle. We were barbequing and boozing when our chopper pilot said that we must saddle up and RTB. There had been a hurricane warning. We sped off back to Airport camp. The powers that be said it was too unsafe to stay in town, instead we were to doss down in the Sgts mess. No probs. We teamed up with our bandit looking mob and drank ourselves silly for three days. Soon we were on our way home. The boys from the SAS exchanged numbers with me and I invited them to the Palladium. Great fun. They looked funny in suits. Life moves on and like all good things they drift away and get filed in the "Those were the days' file. The Falklands War had finished and I wanted to check the whereabouts of Taffy and John. I had lost the numbers but had a photo taken at airport camp. My Roadie Terry said that a SAS bloke drinks in his pub. I asked Terry if he would show him the picture. The SAS man came to Thames TV to see me. His name was JB. He was the strongest man I ever met, and one of the nicest. He looked at the photo and said that the boys were still alive and I should join him on Saturday at the base in Hereford where we would look them up... And so started a relationship with the regiment and the lads, young and old that has lasted till this day.

—JD

39

MEMORIES FROM THE IRANIAN EMBASSY SIEGE, LONDON 1980

Twenty-six hostages were taken (two were murdered) – five terrorists were shot dead and one arrested. We and, I think the rest of Great Britain, were immensely pleased with the outcome of our assault on the Iranian Embassy, Princes Gate, London, in 1980. There has been a lot of debate since regarding the after effects of the UK Special Forces being seen live on television and whether this was a good or bad thing. However, it is a fact and is now history and what is beyond debate is that no other Embassy in London has been attacked since. You tend to block out in your memory most of the bad or mundane parts of your career and only really remember the good or humorous parts. The siege was no exception. Several funny things I remember.

After the siege had finished we were pulled out and regrouped in Regents Park Barracks where sandwiches and beer was supplied. Margaret Thatcher, the Prime Minister, and the then Home Secretary, William Whitelaw came into the room we were in; I was standing talking to three friends as Mrs Thatcher walked down the room towards us. She was obviously going to the front of the room and would be walking straight past our little group. I noticed that one of our four, "Piggy" as he was known and whose politics were slightly right of Attila the Huns and who absolutely adored Mrs T, had not seen her come in. As she approached and went to walk past us I lay my hand on her shoulder guiding her around so she faced our group. I said "Mrs

Thatcher, my friend here regards you as a Goddess" and as I said it, Piggy, a fully seasoned and battle hardened warrior, swung around and saw her for the first time. He then, to our amazement and to his future chagrin, attempted to bow and to really make it worse; it came out as a curtsey! Mrs T was not amused! William Whitelaw addressed all of us and said: "I was standing at the top of the road with your Brigadier, when you chaps went in and there was an enormous explosion and I asked him rather hurriedly "What was that?". He, standing there expressionless, said "it's the men going in through the windows!". Reassured, I continued waiting and a minute or so later, there was another huge explosion. I turned to your Brigadier and without haste asked "and what was that? He shouted "I don't bloody know!" and disappeared. I saw my career flash past my eyes!" My over-riding memory, however, happened a little later; *News at Ten* (ITN) began on the room television showing the assault in graphic detail. At the same time Mrs Thatcher was sitting on the floor talking to Ned K, one of our team – quite a character in his own right. Both were drinking Heineken from a tin and I think Ned was explaining to her how to run the country. Perhaps a lot of the troubles the UK has now are due to the advice Ned gave her! To this day I am not sure who has or had the bigger ego.

—JT

OPERATION NIMROD, THE IRANIAN EMBASSY SIEGE

My squadron was the squadron which took part in and carried out the operation. After a couple of days of waiting in a building a couple of doors down, the question of maintaining fitness cropped up. It was decided that a handful of the team could go for a quick run in the park opposite. At first there were no takers as the troops did not want to be out running as something might happen and they would miss it. Eventually a couple said they would go and did. When they returned they were het up about an attractive female they had seen out running, she had as described by them, a superb pair of large breasts which she had to support with her hands while running. The next day the whole squadron wanted to go running, those not picked sulked.

As the siege dragged on it was decided to split the squadron in half and have a day team and a night team, 12 hours on twelve hours off. Should something happen both halves to join as a whole team. I was in the half that had the night stood down. In the morning we would come together for a handover/takeover briefing/ debriefing. The room used for this was also an eating area. Every morning we would arrive to a devastated scene of leftover food, dirty cups, mugs, cutlery, plates slope and stains. During the handover/takeover I said that my half of the team should be called Operation Nimrod and the other half be known as Operation Dynorod.

At the time just before we carried out the assault we had been watching on television the snooker competition taking place in Sheffield. After the completion of the assault we went back into the holding area from where we were housed. A policeman, who was there and had watched incredulously the assault on television, was asked by one of the team "how's the snooker getting on?"

—SS

40
SURVEILLANCE

Working for a security firm based in London in the 1980s was a really interesting job, varying from Body Guarding the rich and famous in the UK and abroad, to static guarding of property throughout the world. Most of your compatriots were ex Special Forces but not always and some were certainly of the "Walter Mitty" type. Some of the jobs you did were also rather strange.

One summer, I was contacted by an old friend who was running an operation for one of these London Security Firms. He explained that the job would be for three weeks, that there would be a total of twenty-four of us and would consist of carrying out continuous surveillance on a couple of people who were living in Cannes, France. His brief included the fact that the two were Americans who were on the run from the American Inland Revenue, or their equivalent and who had been responsible for an eight million dollar fraud. The FBI was attempting to surreptitiously get a warrant for their extradition from France but apparently it would take three weeks. We were to "check" on them continuously and ensure they stayed in situ.

Three weeks of pure fantasy followed. We were billeted in a five-star hotel in Cannes and in eight man teams we watched the couple. We delivered flowers, occasionally deflating their car tyres (so no quick exit), and making the odd telephone call, etc, to ensure they were still there. We had plenty of free time and Cannes is beautiful: handsome boats and yachts everywhere and beautiful women trying to wear as little as possible.

The surveillance went well: the man and woman were checked on regularly, photographed often and we were quite happy that we had stopped them from going anywhere. We were on excellent money, had excellent accommodation and you could not walk 100 yards without seeing a woman you would die for!

At the end of the third week, the Firms boss came over from London with two FBI Investigators who congratulated us and then went off to see the two culprits.

Two hours later, all twenty-four of us were on a flight back to Heathrow. None of us were feeling too bright. It had been the wrong man and woman!

—JT

41
A COMEDIAN WHO WASN'T IN THE ARMY
JIM DAVIDSON OBE, BELIZE

We came out of the jungle after several weeks patrolling the Guatemalan/Belize Border, had a quick shower and then my mate and I headed for the Sgts Mess in Airport Camp. It had gone 10 P.M. and the barman although actually shutting the bar sold us three crates of Tennents before he left. The two of us began serious drinking. A bloke then walked into the room and headed for the now-closed bar with the obvious intention of getting a drink. He turned to us as he realised there was no barman and my mate recognised him as the comedian Jim Davidson (JD). He invited him to join us and as he did so a typhoon warning came over the speakers in the Mess. It meant we were to close and lock all windows, doors, etc and stay where we were. Two days later, the three of us left the bar, beer-less, starving but firm friends.

THE LONDON PALLADIUM

When we finished our tour in Belize a few months later we returned to the UK. It was nearly Christmas and we found that JD had arranged for Taff, his wife, me and my wife, to go to see his Christmas Panto at the London Palladium. We went by train and were met at Euston by a driver and Rolls Royce and taken to the Palladium in style! At about 4 am we ended up in the Hotel he had booked and paid for. We seem to have drunk with and chatted to most of the UKs Show Business personnel. Not quite the quiet at home we had been planning!

OMAN (1)

Years later, our paths crossed again. I was OC of the Special Task Force, Royal Oman Police and had been in Oman several years. Out of the blue, he rang me and explained he would be performing at the Muscat Novotel the following week and would be arriving the following day. Not to be outdone by his Euston driver and Rolls Royce episode I decided to impress him so the following day when he emerged from the plane at Seeb Airport I was waiting, in full Police uniform. I arrested him immediately, virtually dragging him through customs and immigration and had deposited him in his hotel 20 minutes after landing. His companions arrived a couple of hours later, hot, tired and a little disgruntled. They weren't too impressed with the efficiency of the airport officials but JD was!

OMAN (2)

The next day, my 2IC on the Police Team, took Jim on our Ranges. He fired everything, 9mm pistol, 5.56 Armalite, GPMG, Sterling SMG and then finished it off by throwing grenades. I had various reports about his shooting ability but no-one could fault his "born again soldier" enthusiasm.

OMAN (3)

Before he left Oman we went diving in full sub aqua kit with the help of a friend in the Sultans Navy. Another good day but ruined slightly when Jims diamond encrusted "Rolex" watch filled with water! Unfortunately, he had no warranty given to him by the bloke who had sold him it, for £3000 in a London bar!

WENTWORTH GOLF COURSE

I left Oman in the late 80s and when Jim invited me, my wife and two children to stay at his house bordering Wentworth Golf Course for four days. I had no hesitation in accepting. We spent one day sitting outside, drinking bucks fizz, champagne and orange juice, until Jim decided we should go out to his favourite pub on the A30. We got into his Norwegian Armoured Car, as you do, and set off for the pub. However, his friend who was driving and wearing complete RAF aviator's uniform decided to drive through the golf course. It was extremely funny to see the golfer's expressions when in the middle of Wentworth Golf Course, Jim, wearing a combat jacket and Argentinian helmet and standing in the gunner's position asked them the way to "Port Stanley"!

We had a good night in the pub and on my return to Jim's house I spent most of the remainder of the night in the "Gents" being violently ill. I think the Bucks Fizz had something to do with that.

When I did manage to appear for breakfast, Jim thanked me profusely and after several explanations I found that "two white Russians", who had a previous grievance with Jim, had threatened him in the bar the previous evening. I had apparently sorted it out and the Russians had left. The reason for the really large "Thank Yous" was because they were known to carry knives, and use them! To this day, Jim does not know that I did not know about the knives and that I really couldn't remember anything of the previous night. I was really brave – it is amazing what a drink can do for you! A great character and his generosity to the Military has been rarely recognised.

—JT

42

MARRIED MEN – AND THEIR WIVES

Cpl H brought his wife to the monthly unit do. He tended to hog the bar with his mates and drink a bit too much. His wife, who tended to wear low cut tops and short skirts, would be left alone at the other end of the bar surrounded by young single soldiers admiring the view.

Towards the end of the evening, after too many beers, this situation would cause a row between Cpl H and his wife, usually outside on the unit square. Over many months this developed into a serious domestic where the unit had to be officially involved.

I called Cpl H into my office and explained that this situation could not continue. Things were becoming serious and there was a strong possibility of domestic violence happening. Having laid down the law at length, I lightened the situation and suggested Cpl H might like to spend time with his wife when they attended functions, and, just a suggestion, she might like to dress a little less provocatively. He smiled at me and said OK, sir, but she has got nice t*ts hasn't she?

—DG

43

SOLDIERS - MISBEHAVING

Ordnance Coy, Gutersloh Germany. We had another Pte B in the unit. One of his problems was that his German girlfriend was pregnant and I had to escort Pte B to a German court where he strongly denied that he was the father. DNA tests showed that he was 95% certain to be the father. However, his main problem was that he was an admin burden to the unit. He had also recently been jailed for 28 days for skiving, again. This was the last straw and we decided to give him an admin discharge.

One day his father Mr B 'phoned from UK, unaware of his son's girlfriend and that his son had just done 28 days, complaining bitterly that we were sacking his son.

"He's a good lad" said Mr B, "and I'm going to give him a job". "It's a pity the army can't look after him as he loves the life" Quiet chuckle from my corner. "Oh really Mr B, loves the life does he?" "Yes Capt G" "Well Mr B, if you are going to give him a job that's fine, you obviously know your son much better than I do" "Yes I do Capt G, and I am not impressed that you are sacking him for no good reason". This line of questioning my judgement continued for a few more minutes, with Mr B getting slightly more aggressive each time. Eventually I had had enough. "You think we are sacking your son for no good reason?" "Yes, I do". "Well Mr B, do you know that your son has just spent 28 days in jail?" "Really ? No, I didn't know that Capt G". "Well Mr B, you don't know him quite as well as you thought." Mr B still not very happy, but calmed down slightly.

"Well Capt G, you know what young lads are like". "Yes I do Mr B, especially your young lad". "Well I won't make excuses for him, but I still think you are being rather hard on him". By now, after a good 15 minutes of hassle, I'm getting fed up with Mr B, and decide to educate him and close the conversation with a one liner. "Oh really, Mr B. So you think you really know your son? "Yes I do Capt G" Knowing that Mr B is not aware of his son's German girlfriend, "Well let me congratulate you on becoming a grandfather!" Deafening silence from Mr B.

End of conversation!

—DG

44

HEADQUARTERS BRITISH FORCES HONG KONG

Walking around the headquarters one day, casually chatting to a member of the locally employed Chinese civilian staff.

Somehow the conversation got around to religion and how the headquarters skyscraper block actually housed the forces church.

One Chinese chap, trying to explain he was a Christian, struggled to find the right words and phrases and eventually came out with "Oh no, I'm not a Christian, I'm a Catholic!"

—DG

45
BEING A PARATROOPER

"I know of a clinical trial that I was party to after the Falklands War to see why men would run forward under fire, knowing they were going to die and the mind set with it! We were given a seat and had electrodes put on us, the team asked us how high our pain threshold was and turned the power on slowly increasing the electric pulse to a point when it was no longer bearable.

Thinking that we were competing against each other, we grinned and bore the pain to the maximum. Reeling in our own glory we compared pain levels, only to be told that we now had to go back to the chair and answer questions on a screen, electrodes attached! NOW, what we did not know until that point was for each question we got wrong, a big countdown began on the screen. 10. 9, 8, 7, 6… 0 bang! You got a single jolt at the same level as we had maxed on the initial trial.

The thing about it all was, during the countdown we all began to laugh uncontrollably, something the civvy team found rather strange, that men would laugh knowing they were going to receive pain. This, apparently, went against all previous trials, mainly with the Americans"

—MMM

46

THE OMAN IN THE 1980s
(A SOLDIER IN THE POLICE)

In the early '80s I ran a small British team training the Special Task Force Royal Oman Police in Counter Terrorism. We were based in Muscat and the training included weapon craft, all aspects of siege assault, close quarter combat and of course the basics of being a soldier (although they were policemen!). The Omanis are a very proud race and having never been "colonised" have none of the hang-ups which I have found in other Middle Eastern countries. In fact, the Sheikhs of Oman agreed with Britain in the 19th century to attack any Spanish or French shipping that went past their shores. Britain, in return, promised to help defend Oman if attacked by Spain or France. This was a sort of truce as we both agreed not to attack each other. Surprisingly, this agreement worked. Hence, the naming of the area as the Trucial Oman States. Fairly recently this has been changed to the United Arab Emirates. Working with the Police had many funny moments. One morning driving to work in a police car and wearing full uniform I was waved down by a policeman. He politely explained that I had been speeding and invited me to join a queue of people on the other side of the road. I noticed that all of them were waiting to be dealt with by a lone policeman sitting at a table. I pointed to my uniform and my police car and the man who had stopped me became deeply apologetic and then instantly escorted me to the front of the queue ensuring I was booked first! On another occasion, I left my police car outside the British Airways office in Muscat with my police hat on obvious display. I went in as I was collecting a model aircraft Boeing 737 which we were going to use for assault demonstrations. I was quite pleased with my trophy when leaving their office and heading for the car. Unfortunately, however, there was no car! After a half hour fruitless search and fractionally before I reported my police car stolen, a policeman on a bike appeared and explained the police had towed it away. A bit of an achievement as it had been locked. There was no indication that it was a no parking area and there were at least 20 odd other vehicles parked randomly on the street. I asked him why this was and where were any signs. He shrugged, smiled and explained that the signs would be going up the following week! The Omanis loved sport and particularly football so being a fervent Liverpool supporter I invited the Team to watch the videos I had sent out from the UK of Liverpool's matches. Our four-man British Team lived in a small house on a hill overlooking Muscat. A beautiful location but a little crowded at weekends when 60 Omani policemen and we four Brits would watch the match. I would probably already know the result but I never let them know beforehand. When I left the Team, three years later, I had total faith in them. Whether they were brilliant as a Counter Terrorism Team I would let the Omani hierarchy judge, but I do know that they all spoke English with a strong "scouse" accent and all of them supported Liverpool Football Club! When I first arrived in Oman and joined the Police Team, I was sitting in the Police Club when I spotted another newcomer sitting at the bar. I started chatting to him and found his story really fascinating. 15 years before he had been a British Policeman on loan to Oman and was helping the police to reorganise in Salalah. A war was taking place with North Yemenese attempting to invade and take over Oman starting with the southern area of Salalah.

Whilst on duty he had come across a wounded Lcpl and he helped him get medical help and generally looked after him. Apparently the Omani never forgot this and the kindness of the English Policeman. The Omani prospered and after transferring to the police eventually became the Chief of Police Oman. He had then searched for and contacted the English Policeman and had asked him to come back to the Oman and join the police there as a full colonel! As the bloke had retired from the British Police several years before and was pottering around in his garden in Surrey, he jumped at the chance. Thus he was back in the Oman. A lovely story but it had a sequel. Three years later when I was finishing with the Omani Police and about three weeks before I actually left the Training Team, one of my Lieutenants, who I had personally taught, particularly on the use of the 9mm Browning pistol, was involved in an incident on the Saudi/Oman border. He and his driver had come across some whisky smugglers and had chased their vehicle along the border but had then been ambushed. Saif's driver was killed but Saif returned automatic fire and then approached the Saudi Toyota which by then was burning and which he assumed had been abandoned. As he neared the vehicle a Saudi stepped out from behind it and emptied a Kalashnikov at him.

He was hit seven times and went down in a heap. The Saudi came over to finish him off but Saif, who had managed to draw his Browning pistol from his lying down position, had "double-tapped", the whiskey smuggler hitting him twice in the head which killed the Saudi outright. Up until then Saif had done everything wrongly but had come out of it the winner. He had been very very lucky. Two rounds fell out of his mouth when we were putting him in the casevac helicopter but none of the seven rounds had hit in any vital organ.

The week before I left I went to see him in Muscat Hospital and he was sitting up in bed. He was very happy and extremely pleased to see us. His first words to me were to thank us for all the hours we had spent teaching him and the Teams, the use of the Browning pistol, the "Double Tap" and shooting from various unusual positions. He did not know that I, in fact, was going to give him a minor bollocking for all the errors he had made during the incident but as Saif was talking to me I remembered the British Full Colonel I had met in the Police Club three years before.. "Saif" I said, "what a fantastic thing you have done, you will, no doubt, move up in the police ranks as you are already becoming a legend! Please do not forget me if you make it to the Chief of Police position" I went on "No matter when that is or where I am in the UK, please phone me and offer me Brigadier or something equivalent in your future police force!" I finished by adding "You will not have to ask me twice!" I am now seventy years old and still awaiting that phone call – at this rate I may well end up the oldest Police Brigadier, or its equivalent, in the World!

—JT

47

THE FALKLANDS – PASS ROYAL!

A party of Sappers were moving up from Green Beach to establish a Harrier base on the ridge above and were being led by a guide from the RE Commando Squadron past an area occupied by helicopters from the RNAS. It was pitch black and suddenly from ahead came the challenge "Halt! Who goes there?" This was delivered in the shaky manner only employed by non soldiers and so the guide concluded that this was about the second most dangerous object on earth... A sailor with a gun. The party froze and the challenge was followed by half of a password that meant nothing to us and the unmistakeable sound of a Sub Machine Gun (SMG) being cocked. The guide hissed back into the night..." I haven't got a bloody clue what you're talking about mate... But if you point that bloody gun at me I'll take it off you... Shove it up your arse, and pull the trigger!" Brief pregnant paused followed by a relieved sounding "Pass Royal!" NOTE the sailor's nickname for a Royal Marine (Or indeed anybody with a green beret) is 'Royal!'

—CW

48

PHYSICAL TRAINING ON RFA SIR BEDIVERE – STAR JUMPS

ON the run south from Ascension Island to the Falklands we were embarked on a very crowded Landing ship the RFA 'Sir Bedivere' The ship was overcrowded and making full speed through the 'Roaring Forties' but even so fitness training had to continue. The ship was heaving up and down by anything up to 20 feet at the bow and stern and during one notable PT session on the flight deck at the stern led by our PTI 'Sparky', he was demonstrating the next exercise 'Star jumps'. At the precise moment he jumped and flung his arms and legs out wide, the ship dropped away underneath him leaving him far higher in the air than he had ever been. His eyes became saucers as in a split second he realised that he was now dropping while several thousand tons of ship were coming back up to meet him!

Oh the merriment of it all! The PT sessions from then included all the exercises that didn't entail leaving the ground!

—CW

IN THE 1990s

49

WHEN ONE'S HEAD IS ON THE BLOCK

When the MOD procurement signalled me in Brunei and told me to sell off the four SCOUT Helicopters that were being replaced by BELL I thought it would be reasonably straightforward. The Foreign Office when asked for advice were quick to point out that they must not be sold in flying condition as there was always the worry that someone would fly into the Palace and attempt to assassinate the Sultan. This was years before 9/11. I duly got financial authority from the Bruneian Treasury to dispose of what was in effect one of their assets and directed the Aviation Flight to render the aircraft unserviceable. They were sold at auction for a miserable sum – about B$600 (About £260 then) I think, ostensibly for scrap.

I was en route to UK for a meeting when I had a telephone call in my hotel room in Hong Kong. It was my chum Will Mellows who opened with "Did you sell some helicopters?" I could but assent. "Well" he said ominously, "the Bruneian Special Branch wants a word with you".

On my return to Brunei after a few days in UK worrying about what I had started, I was sent for by the British High Commission to discuss the problem with the First Secretary.

Everybody seemed generally on my side but made it clear that if the Bruneians kicked up, my head was on the block. In due course via the BHC I was 'invited' with my Commanding Officer and the First Sec to attend at the Prime Minister's Office for a Royal Ass Kicking. I say Royal because in Brunei the Sultan is also the Prime Minister.

A Bruneian Government helicopter was sent for us and we landed in the Palace Gardens. We were met amenably and shown into an inner office where we were met by the Sultan's Senior Aides and Head of Security. We sat around a low table and were served teas and soft drinks (a Muslim Country of course) and trays of gorgeous sweet and sticky cakes which kept coming. The conversations were very friendly and ran for about three quarters of an hour about the world, the weather, Liverpool Football Club – anything but the subject of my discomfort. Then suddenly the great man made an oblique allusion to the sin for which I was being arraigned and produced with a flourish, a sheaf of photographs of the a/c in a local scrap yard. The Flight had, by puncturing the tanks and removing the control columns rendered them, by the critically high H&S standards of UK, un-flyable. The third world of course, has other ideas. As he was putting it over the wiles of the average mechanic would soon get these flying again.

My CO jumped in swiftly and overwhelmed him with, quite simply, bluff! After more tea and cakes, and much hands shaking we were flown home. I was relieved, and confused and stuffed with sweet cake.

I CAN say, if you ever have to receive a Royal Bollocking, look for a benign regime in which to do it.

—GC

50
DIVING WITH GADGET MAN

During a unit sub aqua diving trip to the Mediterranean our team of eight very experienced divers shared a hired dive boat with a similar sized group of Germans. We tended to favour basic wet suits with tee shirts and had some very basic but very well cared for kit. One or two had basic dive computers but most relied on diving watches and dive tables to work out dive durations and depth profiles etc. On deck we always carried out the same drills and buddy checks and had a good two weeks of trouble free diving down to our maximum of 50 metres. The Germans never tired of scoffing at us and demonstrating their array of brand new, state of the art, gadgets and computers as well as their lightweight dry suits complete with anti shark hoods and gloves. They really looked the business and we began to be a bit miffed! Once out at sea we usually dived two separate areas and were a week into the diving when we discovered that they had not ventured below about 15 metres. On the only day we dived at the same site my buddy and I were surfacing from about 25 metres after a long dive and saw a German pair above us at the safety stop of six metres. We came up level with them and the German leader went through a whole routine of checking his watch, computer, dive timer and gauges etc before giving me a sarcastic sign and heading for the surface at speed. Too bad he didn't have a boat detector amongst his gismos though, since he banged head first into the hull of our 30 ton dive boat in a very good impression of a torpedo! He and his team were mortified when we underequipped Brits rescued him, got him aboard and applied First Aid. Sad to say, no beers were forthcoming and while his team went back to a swish hotel we went cheerily back to our camp site via the bar!

—CW

51
DIVING GALLIPOLI

As a last jaunt and treat to myself before retiring from the Regular Army I organised a diving expedition to the Dardanelles region of Turkey and the Gallipoli battlefields. The stated aim was to have a look at, and replace the white ensigns on, two British battleships sunk during the campaign on the 80th anniversary of their loss. Unfortunately the use of the phrase 'survey the wrecks' in our paperwork raised some doubts amongst the Turkish military authorities who have, to their credit, preserved the battlefield of ANZAC bay as a national memorial to both their own and our servicemen who fought and died there. In order to ensure we kept on the straight and narrow they would send a small naval patrol boat out with our locally hired craft every time we dived. This made our Turkish crew very nervous since the Turkish authorities are not renowned for going easy on people who break the rules. Whenever we surfaced at the end of a dive we would theatrically wave our hands at the unsmiling bloke with a Machine Gun on the bows of the patrol boat to show we had brought nothing up from the bottom. While a battlefield tour on land is impressive, with all the trenches still visible, it is underwater in the shallows that the detritus of the Gallipoli campaign is still clearly evident. From the great groove in the sand where the steamer 'River Clyde' ran aground to the sunken small craft, landing craft, equipment and even human remains scattered along the ANZAC and Suvla bays. For the soldier, an unforgettable and moving experience.

—CW

IN THE NEW MILLENIUM

52

FALKLANDS RETURN 2008 – MISTAKEN IDENTITY

I was fortunate to be given a place on the flight back to the Falkland Islands in November 2008. This had been arranged by the South Atlantic Medal Association 1982 (SAMA82) which made most of the arrangements and which does so much for the veterans and UK/FIs relations. There were perhaps 30 of us and we were all instructed to get to Heathrow and meet up with the organisers there. It was very much a mixed bag of ex-PARA, Marine, Special Forces, Guards and relatives of some servicemen who had not made it back in 1982. Obviously at that stage, few of us knew each other and we were seated all over the plane for the long flight to Stanley. I fell asleep after we boarded and on feeling the plane landing I stood up, got my rucksack from the locker above my head and waited to disembark. I then noticed I was the only one standing! As I was wondering whether to sit down or not, the door on the opposite side of the plane to me, opened and three rather swarthy looking men appeared and began looking for their seats. At that moment a loud laugh resounded throughout the plane. We had actually landed temporarily at Punto Arenas and some wit had said "My God, we're trading three of theirs for one of ours."

A serious postscript to the above The Argentinian cemetery, which the three Argentinians were visiting, is a beautifully laid out area with many graves not far from Goose

Green. Unfortunately, the Argentinian Government frowns on their Nationals visiting it so there are not that many visitors. These three were an obvious exception.

—JT

" The Captain was just remarking on your bravery for taking this flight to Buenos Aires, when your mates all went Tristar to Mount Pleasant..!"

53

I SOLD MY MEDALS YESTERDAY

I sold my medals yesterday,
It hurt but I was strong,
With all the mounting debts through age,
I knew it wasn't wrong.

I sold my medals yesterday,
I am 70 this year,
There won't be many more parades for me,
So really I don't care.

I sold my medals yesterday,
They have gone and that's a fact,
I am really so very happy,
As I can make sure the roofs intact.

I sold my medals yesterday,
It was on Dickinsons Real Deal,
I had my 15 minutes of fame,
But now it seems unreal.

I sold my medals yesterday,
Did I actually go through with it?
I must have done, they're not around
And boy I feel like s**t!

—JT

54
SOLD AND GONE!

Lot 563, 13 Sep 12

Category:
CAMPAIGN GROUPS AND PAIRS

Estimate:
£8,000-£12,000
Hammer Price:
£17,000

Description:
 The superb 'Operation Nimrod' and 'Operation Corporate' group of five awarded to Warrant Officer J. V. Thompson, Special Air Service, formerly Royal Army Ordnance Corps, whose unique and extraordinary service saw him present during two of the 'The Regiment's' most successful operations of the modern era, encompassing both the Iranian Embassy Siege in May 1980 as one of the four members of 'A' Squadron attached to what was a 'B' Squadron operation, and then two years later, as a result of his changing squadrons from 'A' to 'G' he took part in this Squadron's covert intelligence gathering operations during the Falklands War, which saw his four-man patrol embedded on the Island some three weeks prior to the allied invasion – as it turned out had he remained with his old

squadron he would have missed the Falklands War altogether as they were kept back on home duties

U.N. Medal, Cyprus; General Service 1962, 1 clasp, Northern Ireland (23739193 Sgt J. V. Thompson RAOC); South Atlantic 1982, with rosette (23739193 Cpl J. V. Thompson RAOC (SAS)); Regular Army L.S. & G.C., E.II.R. (23739193 WO1 J V Thompson RAOC); Republic of Korea Service Medal, mounted court style as worn, generally nearly extremely fine (5).

Footnote

John Vincent Thompson enlisted into the Royal Electrical Mechanical Engineers Junior Leaders in 1959, aged 17, taking up his man service the following year. He successfully completed his parachute training, and, staying with the R.E.M.E. joined the Parachute Brigade in 1962, being posted to Cyprus on New Year's Day 1964.

He was amongst the first British Paras to remove their red berets and exchange them for the light blue beret of the United Nations, when the U.N. took over responsibility for peacekeeping operations in Cyprus on 27 March 1964.

Thompson transferred to the Royal Army Ordnance Corps, Parachute Brigade in 1969 and five years later in 1974, together with his Brigadier, gained the rare distinction of being presented at a parade with the Republic of Korea Service Medal on the completion of a one-year posting in Korea on a Commonwealth Liaison Mission.

In 1978 he successfully applied for and completed his S.A.S. selection and was posted to Boat Troop, 'A' Squadron.

Operation Nimrod

On the morning of 30 April 1980 six armed gunmen took 26 people hostage at the Iranian Embassy in South Kensington. As a result a coded message was sent to S.A.S. H.Q. in Hereford requesting immediate assistance and 'B' Squadron, whose turn it was to act as the Counter-Terrorism Team were soon rushed to the scene. Thompson's own involvement in the Siege happened quite by chance three days later when 'B' Squadron requested additional support. Thompson and three of his 'A' Squadron colleagues happened to be leaving camp on their way to watch Liverpool play Arsenal in a third replay of the F.A. Cup semi-final, when an M.O.D. Policeman stopped them and told them that they were to attach themselves to "B' Squadron for the duration of the siege with immediate effect. They were taken to London by a Chinook helicopter and at the time were not at all impressed at missing the football match.

Two days later, on 5th May 1980 at 19:24hrs, following the shooting by the terrorists of one of the hostages the fifty-five men of the S.A.S. began their rescue mission. Thompson and his three 'A' Squadron colleagues were split into two pairs and assigned the important role of assaulting the front and rear of the building from the ground level. Thompson and his partner were given the front of the building where they successfully fired numerous gas canisters through the four first floor windows.

He and his partner had to be alert and ready at all times for the terrorists in case they tried try to shoot their way out of the building, and in the actual event had to deal with various guns and hand grenades that were thrown out of the windows by the terrorists as well as deal with the hostage reception. The raid lasted 17 minutes in total and by the end of it five of the six terrorists were dead. One hostage was killed by the terrorists in the raid and two others wounded.

The following year Thompson transferred from Boat Troop, 'A' Squadron to Boat Troop, 'G' Squadron, a somewhat fortuitous move as it turned out for an elite soldier seeking action, as the following year his old squadron were destined not to take part in the Falklands Conflict being kept back in the essential roll of homeland security.

The Falklands

During the Falklands War Thompson with the rest of 'G' Squadron were inserted by helicopter at night in four-man patrols, some three weeks prior to the invasion. Thompson's Patrol Commander was awarded an M.M. for this action and his citation which was published in the London Gazette gives detail of their mission:

"Inserted by helicopter from the Naval Task Force at a distance of 120 miles from the islands, he maintained observations of the enemy movement and dispositions in the Bluff Cove, West Stanley areas for a period of twenty-eight days. In a totally hostile environment, with the only protection from ground and air search provided by the skill and stealth of his patrol, the reporting was both accurate and timely.

In order to obtain the detail of the enemy disposition he was required to move his observation position to close and often obvious positions to gain the intelligence required. This he did with great courage and skill knowing that if compromised his patrol could not have been extracted from any predicament caused by enemy action. In addition he communicated his information in an environment where the enemy were known to possess a Direction Finding capability."

Following the success of this mission Thompson was employed in fighting patrols for the duration of the conflict.

As well as the M.M. to his Patrol Commander, one other member of his four-man patrol received an M.I.D.

Warrant Officer I John Vincent Thompson left the Special Air Service on 13 January 1983, aged 40 on completion of 23 years and 77 days service. He immediately took up a job in the Royal Oman Police Special Task Force and also the Sultan's Special Force Oman, with whom he served in the rank of Major between 1983 and 1988.

On returning to the UK he was active in the security industry, involved in the close protection of several well-known personalities, until retiring at 65. During the last five years, he has remained reasonably fit by becoming a 1st Dan Black Belt in Martial Arts, a National Swimming Lifeguard, running several marathons, including the London and Snowdonia, and walking up to Everest Base Camp, earning reasonable amounts for charities.

" I must admit that I hadn't realised that two years National Service at Chipping Sodbury was so ..Erm.. Dangerous!"

55

FALKLANDS RETURN 2008 – WITH THE GUARDS

We watched the two Welsh Guardsmen go to the cliff edge and throw their poppies over the *Galahads* final resting place. The two of them had kept themselves very much to themselves during the first three days of the trip back to the Falklands which SAMA82 (The South Atlantic Medal Association), had organised.

The four 2PARA men and I could not help but see how much actually being there was affecting them emotionally. They were obviously crying and not a little embarrassed. One of the 2PARA blokes decided to do something about it.

As the two Welshmen drew level with us the 2PARA bloke offered them a cigarette each, they stopped, gratefully took them and lit them. One of the Paras then suggested they look at their cigarette. Neatly inscribed on both were: "As always, scrounged from 2PARA." They had to laugh!

Brilliant – Ice broken – It is the little things that matter!

—JT

" Trust me Senor… Now would be a very
bad time to start your demonstration!"

56

THE NOBEL PEACE PRIZE 1991 (AND WHERE'S OUR MONEY?)

I see that Aung San Suu Kyi's Nobel peace Prize of 1991, but only more recently claimed, came with the whacking sum of $1.3 million. I wonder what that is in Drachmas.

Being a good Buddhist soul (or as the unlamented Georgie Bush would have said, 'a good Christian Buddhist'), she decided to sink it into the health and welfare of the Burmese people, so long overlooked. What an absolute gem!

It will however come as a shock to most that I, Crossland of No Fixed Abode, share with this famous lady, the honour of having been awarded the Nobel Peace Prize. I guess that makes me a Nobel Laureate – sounds good!

'LIES!' I hear you all shout. 'RUBBISH!' You bawl. Yes, of course, I would expect such a pointed response from all my chums. 'CHARLATAN' Well you all know me, yes, generally a fair charge, but not over this. I am a genuine winner of this August award. How So? In rooting through the history of Alfred's Prestigious Awards, have discovered that in 1988, the Nobel Committee felt it appropriate to bestow the distinction on all "United Nations Peacekeepers" that is, all the blue beret troops dating back to the start of the UN Peacekeeping Ops. That makes at least tens of thousands of international soldiers who have donned the Blue Beret – and haven't a clue that someone in Oslo has noticed. Interestingly, UN Troops – less The British – draw UN Pay along with their National recompense. The Brits (well, our Masters) decided we don't need such venal tempting to stand duty, unlike all the Scandinavians for instance who are all short term volunteers signed up specifically for one lucrative UN Tour. Nice one Britannia, screwed us again!

So going back to the Dynamite Inheritance, the portion of the Brigade that went to Cyprus in 1964, 1 PARA, Bde HQ and others, must also qualify for this great award, after all, did the UN not take over control of the operation and all therein? Did you who were there not eschew your Beret, Maroon, Airborne, Swanking For The Use Of, for the jolly powder puff copy of the Army Air Corps' mincing chapeau? (Some of us got a cravat thrown in as part of the package, though why I know not as I never saw anyone wearing one).

Maybe we should all band together and march on the UN HQ demanding to know where the cash is that went with our Award. After all, somebody got it! And I never got to do an Acceptance Speech, you know the form… "I'd like to thank me mudder, Father O'Reilly, my Scoutmaster, my mate in nine Sqn and… YAWN!"

—GC

57

ALWAYS A LITTLE FURTHER BUT NOT TOO FAR – EVEREST 2010

In November 2010, 20 ex Special Forces soldiers, average age around the 60 mark walked up to Everest Base Camp. It was extremely enjoyable, very much like being thirty again. We made a lot of money for Help for Heroes – the soldier's charity and when we came back to the UK after the three weeks or so we all felt we had done a little bit more than the normal man of that age. When at the Base Camp and looking up at the final third of the mountain I thought of all the people who have managed to get to the top and survived and what an achievement it is. I went to a Parachute Brigade in Leicester several months later with about twenty of us with our wives. After several beers I explained the idea that I had had to form a team to tackle the mountain. I suggested to the other ex-Airborne blokes that if enough showed interest I would look into sponsorship for an attempt on the final third. Funnily enough, the more we drank the more feasible it became and the more interested everyone seemed to be. On returning home from the Reunion I emailed the whole group asking them to confirm their interest. In the cold light of day, things change! Four did not answer, eight said "No" emphatically, two volunteered for Base Camp and six inferred I was insane! Getting old is a terrible thing!

—JT

58
I WANT MY COLD WAR BACK

Maybe I'm going through one of those stages of life where it's better to remember the past than it is to look to the future. But you see I want the Cold War back; it just seemed a better era than what we have today.

When two different political cultures faced each other over a clear line drawn across Europe and observers stared at each other across No Man's Land wondering what the other was thinking; when the threat of aggressive action from either side was so alarming that it's extent could never be gauged because we all knew that it would all end in tears and all end in worldwide catastrophe. When foot soldiers from both sides of the walled divide spent their entire lives painting out-dated and mechanically useless equipment, drinking copious amounts of cheap alcohol or playing somewhat pointless war games whilst scientists with heads made of Teflon created ever more powerful buckets of sunshine to rain down on each other.

So why do I miss it? Because the World was a safer place then, nobody cared much for Islamic extremists, the Middle/Near/Far East were simply areas of this planet that were kept under communist control or bribed to steer clear from the teachings of Lenin. They posed no real threat to the stability of our lives even as the mighty Soviet Empire battled with renegade Afghans. Britain policed the Micks in a cat and mouse game and America marched up and down along the line drawn across the Koreas.

So I want my Cold War back. OK, I cannot have the original so I want Cold War II. I want the Old Guard back in power in the Kremlin with the tanks rolling through Warsaw, Prague and Budapest. I want to see the Soviet armies re-established and good old commie bricklayers hard at work building that wall. Take me back to a time when we didn't need Europe united by a trading Market or a common currency; when everyone in Western Europe had their own currency, their own Army and their own border controls; when everyone in Europe were united by fear and the need to defend rather than the need for petty bureaucracy. That way all the "essential" Polish workers can be sent home and the Big Issue doesn't need to be sold by the Romanian homeless; we don't have to suffer Russian ownership of everything from football clubs to essential services; we can have our crime home-grown and taken out of the hands of Eastern Europeans and placed firmly in the control of suited East End villains, psychotic Glaswegians and mental Mancunians; no longer will we have to tolerate stabbings from Kosovans or Albanians although we might return to the more intriguing scenario of a Bulgarian being stabbed in the arse with a poisoned brolly and we might have our fruit picked by Englishmen and women rather than hordes of Eastern European gypsies.

So there you go. I want my Cold War back. Or rather I want Cold War two. Not that the MoD are likely to call me up as an essential element in the defence of Europe. FFS I'm a semi-invalid eight days from my 50th birthday! So maybe I really want Cold War two followed by the previously anticipated WW three. No nukes mind but Soviet Shock Armies sweeping through Germany, Scandinavia, the Lowlands and France, (especially France)… And then I can don those old combats, denims, woolly pully and the fifty-eight webbing that I cannot find in my heart to put on Ebay. I might not be called upon to fight a retreat off the beaches of France but I somehow see myself as a Dad's Army Sgt resplendent in 80s gear and armed with an old SLR brought out of stock. A last line of defiance in a much missed conflict that failed to materialise before!

But that's probably because I have been drinking again!

—K13eod

59

GETTING THERE IN THE END!

I left school at eighteen and joined Coutts & Co, bankers to the Royal Family and the Aristocracy, in the West End. One day, aged twenty-four, when gazing out of an upper window onto the Strand, I was shocked suddenly to have a clear vision of my life leading direct to my 65th birthday, and retirement. You could call it my Yellow Brick Road moment! But instead of there being a wondrous journey, with amazing twists and turns, and a fantastical Wizard (or whatever) at the end, I saw only a straight line. Although I would have been secure and, no doubt, content in a settled-down, middle-class, suburban sort of way, I thought, as I looked down at the people below, what will I have done with my life, with no experiences or memories worth thinking and talking about? But there were two problems. My loving parents, and my good and tolerant employer who had me in mind for bigger and better things. How could I get out of this benign rut and at the same time keep their goodwill?

The fact that I cared about this shows how hidebound by convention I was. The answer, as I saw it, presented itself one day when I saw an advertisement in *The Times* for young men to apply for a Short Service Commission. Perfect, I thought. I'll apply, get accepted, and win the praise and admiration of all for such a splendid and patriotic change of life. I duly filled in the form and was instructed to appear before a Regular Commissions Board, and three days assessment at Westbury in Wiltshire. I took some of my holiday entitlement and lied to family and the bank that I was going abroad. And to my astonishment, despite having appalling long hair, and no cub, scout, or military experience whatsoever, I passed, and discovered later that I was one of only a tiny handful of successful candidates on that particular course! I was told to report to an office in Berkeley Square for further instructions. And later I was given a joining date at the RMA, Sandhurst. Brilliant, I can now confront my parents and employer with pride. But oh dear! My father descended into one of his regular depressions; my mother couldn't quite grasp what was going on; while my manager told me in no uncertain terms what a bloody fool I was, and that if I thought bank life and discipline was difficult, it was nothing compared with the military life upon which I was about to embark. I think all this made me even more determined, for that Yellow Brick Road of mine wasn't going to go away.

I will condense the next part of the story because, with the full blessing of the authorities, I didn't join the Army straight away. I had told them I first wanted to see the world after a cocooned life, and so could I delay my start date? They thought this was a good idea. A more rounded officer. So, by molasses tanker out of Liverpool, Greyhound bus, hitch-hike, trains, more boats, planes, and foot, I saw the world for a year, working in bars, on fishing boats, and on any site that would employ me to keep me going. The year was 1972. Happy days it was on 1st January 1973 that I at last presented myself at Sandhurst a completely changed human being. So changed – and I must continue to shorten this story – that on a fine day in May, having been given a withering dressing down by my platoon and company commanders, and told by the giant of an Adjutant that I had been a complete waste of time and money, I was marched into the Commandant's office for my final interview and leaving instructions. A friend then drew up outside Mons

College, loaded my bag for me, and took me to his flat in Richmond where I spent the next few weeks in a deep depression and virtual silence. My parents thought I was still at Camberley. One day my friend had had enough. Did I intend spending the rest of my life like this? Get a job, for Christ's sake. So I joined an industrial agency and started to work again. I picked, packed, laboured, loaded, dug, drove, and clerked... day in, day out, night in, night out. And eventually the Sandhurst memories faded. So much so that by the beginning of 1975 I found myself on the agency's inside, and responsible for the entire Greater London operation. But the devil got into me again. There were still two important things I had to do with my life. I didn't want to work for some other man, making his money for him. And I wanted to turn the tables on those who had tried, and nearly succeeded, to finish me off. Why hadn't they simply said, "Look – we really don't think you're cut out for this. Shift ho and try something else." But that's not the way of the world. They had to have their pound of flesh and make an example of me. The term Annus Mirabilis is not always understood. But they do exist. 1975 was such a year. It was make or break. First, I had long nurtured a desire to work for myself so I incorporated my own recruitment business that spring. And second, I had discovered an organisation in the Kings Road, Chelsea, which I had first heard about from my old Colour Sergeant, Robbie Robertson, CG – one of the good guys. This was the Special Air Service. I had also discovered that you could actually join this Regiment and remain a civilian. Was not this – working for myself, doing Selection, and starting a parallel career in the TA SAS – absolute very Heaven? Apart from the extra delight of later marrying one of my staff, you bet it was! After passing all the joining tests at the Duke of York's I said to the sergeant, with a final nod to my old cautious ways, that I had just started a business and would it not be better to delay my Selection course? He replied bluntly that it was up to me but if I was serious about joining the Regiment I should proceed on both fronts at the same time. If not, I may as well leave. That was it. I did just as he said. And somehow it all worked out. Thanks buddy, whoever you were. I had many motivations on Selection; patriotism, loathing of both communist and right-wing ideologies. The desire to serve. The need to prove myself fit and capable. Not wanting to let my new friends, and the PSIs, down. But I'm human enough to admit that I was also motivated by the desire to make amends. I recall the names of those people even now. Though they would never know what became of their object of loathing, whenever I topped the Fan for the umpteenth time, and I knew that I was going to succeed, I always muttered dark words about them to myself! I had made it, despite them, and had seldom been happier. My parents lived on into their 80s and 90s content that their six children had all worked out. In 2008, I was able to pass on the business to my colleagues after thirty-three years of hard, see-sawing, nerve-jangling, slog. I am also lucky to have a good family life with four grandchildren. But above all I am so proud to have lived and soldiered with some of the best and most extraordinary people on Earth. I have mixed with Originals, 1st & 2nd, Belgian & French, Maquis and Resistance, men from the Forties to the Noughties – Regular, TA and Reserve. Not many people can say that. I only hope that they have all regarded me in the same way that I regard and honour them.

—Anon

60

PARA v MARINE

A group of Paras and Marines are sitting around bragging about their different services. One of the Marines says "You know of course, the Marines invented sex." They all pondered this statement, until one of the Para blokes replied:
"Yes, but the Paras introduced it to women!"

—Anon Aldershot.

A SIGN OF THE TIMES: "An old (anonymous, he is probably reading this) Vigilant Platoon, 16 Para Bde, member told me that he went to the first Vigilant Platoon Reunion in Blackpool and was dropped off by his wife. He asked her to wait around the corner in case he didn't take to the get together.

Shortly after, he reappeared and got into the car, "What's wrong?" asked his wife. "The place is full of old, fat, bald headed men" he replied.

"Look in the mirror" she came back."

—GC

LOST IN THE TRANSLATION! "I was driving through Staffordshire with a chum who had done a couple of Hong Kong tours. We passed the sign for Her Majesty's Young Offenders Institution near Lichfield. We drove on in silence and Brian, a former Paymaster, was clearly deep in thought. "You have a large Chinese Community here?" he asked.

"I don't know," I replied, "perhaps."

More silence.

Brian finally spoke. "I wonder what HM YOI means in English?"

—GC